❖•❖•❖•❖•❖•❖•❖•❖•❖•❖•❖•❖•❖•❖•❖•❖•❖•❖•❖

FRANKENSTEIN

❖•❖•❖•❖•❖•❖•❖•❖•❖•❖•❖•❖•❖•❖•❖•❖•❖•❖•❖

TERROR STALKS THE NIGHT!

Frankenstein woke from his sleep with horror; a cold perspiration covered his forehead, his teeth chattered, and every limb trembled—and then, by the dim and yellow light of the moon as it forced its way through the shutters, he saw the monster. It moved heavily across the room, coming toward him—the miserable thing he had created.

Frankenstein waited in horror. The monster pushed wider the curtains of the bed. His eyes, if eyes they could be called, were fixed on Frankenstein. The monster's jaws opened, and he muttered some strange, hoarse sounds, while a grin wrinkled his cheeks. . . . The monster stretched out his hand. . . .

FRANKENSTEIN

BASED ON THE NOVEL BY MARY SHELLEY

Adapted by Dale Carlson
Cover Illustration by Tom Nachreiner

 **GOLDEN PRESS**

Western Publishing Company, Inc.

Racine, Wisconsin

Contents

The Creation 1

IT WAS A DARK, stormy night late in November. In his laboratory, a tower room high over the roofs of Ingolstadt, Germany, Dr. Victor Frankenstein bent over the huge, lifeless figure before him. It was nearly finished, this creature that had occupied his mind and soul for almost two years. In an agony of excitement, Frankenstein examined his work. Finished! All that remained was to infuse the spark of life into its lifeless form, to apply his electrical instruments and make his creature live.

Frankenstein performed his final task and waited, his gaze fixed on the gigantic figure. It was already one in the morning; the rain battered against the window of his laboratory. His candle was nearly burned out, when, by the glimmer of its pale light, he saw the dull yellow eye of the creature open; it breathed hard, and a violent shudder shook its limbs.

Frankenstein stared, horrified, at this catastrophe, this hideous thing he had worked on so hard and had taken such pains to form. The creature's body, though huge, was

11

in perfect proportion, and Frankenstein had chosen his features as beautiful. Beautiful! Ugh! His yellow skin barely covered the muscles and arteries beneath. His hair was thick and shiny black, his teeth of a pearly whiteness, but the handsome hair and teeth only made a horrid contrast with his watery eyes—which seemed almost the same color as the yellowish sockets in which they were set—his shriveled skin and straight black lips.

"Oh, God!" thought Frankenstein. "How changeable are the feelings of human nature. I've worked hard for nearly two years, for the sole purpose of infusing life into an inanimate body. My dream was to prove that I had discovered the secret of life, to create a new race of beings. For this I've gone without rest, without family and friends. Now I've finished, and I can't bear the sight of him!"

The beauty of Frankenstein's dream had vanished. After one last look, filled with breathless horror and disgust, he rushed out of the laboratory to his bedroom and threw himself, still clothed, onto the bed. He hoped for sleep, for a few moments of forgetfulness. Sleep did come, but with it came wild, frightening dreams.

He saw himself first as a boy, with his family, in their lovely Swiss home in Geneva, where Frankenstein was born. He saw his father, a man of honor and great importance, respected by all who knew him; his mother, now dead, but in life, gentle and beautiful; his two younger brothers, Ernest and William; and Elizabeth, the lovely Elizabeth, adopted into the family as a child and adored by them all.

Even as a boy, Victor Frankenstein had a passionate thirst for knowledge. While Elizabeth took pleasure in beauty, in the majestic and wondrous scenes that surrounded their Swiss home, Victor was not satisfied with the appearances of things. He had to find out their causes. The world to him was a secret he had to discover, and his earliest memory was his own curiosity, his need to learn the hidden laws of nature.

The family's favorite home was not their house in the town, but their country house at Belrive on the eastern shore of Lake Geneva. Here Victor read and studied, choosing for company only his family and his closest school friend, Henry Clerval. Victor desired only to learn, though not about all things. Politics, government, and languages bored him. It was the secrets of heaven and earth he was after, and whether he studied the outward substance of things or the inner spirit of nature and the mysterious soul of man, his curiosity was always about the world's physical secrets. His childhood was a happy one, with his books, his loving Elizabeth, and the close bonds of friendship he formed with Henry Clerval.

Frankenstein, in the darkness of his bedroom, dreamed on. His mind held the picture of his family as they were, with himself happy among them, for a few more seconds before he saw himself on that fatal day.

They were all at their summer home at Belrive when they witnessed a violent and terrible thunderstorm. Frankenstein was fifteen years old and had, until then, learned much of his natural philosophy from sixteenth-century writers such as Agrippa, who wrote of magic; Paracelsus, the alchemist and chemist; and Albertus Magnus, the thirteenth-century scholastic philosopher. How was young

Frankenstein to know that their ancient principles had been entirely exploded, that there was now a more modern system of science? His father was not scientific, and Frankenstein was left to struggle to teach himself these difficult subjects, which were not taught in the schools of Geneva. He searched these books for a way to find the elixir of life, tried to raise ghosts and devils through their incantations, and floundered through their ancient theories—until the accident of the thunderstorm changed everything.

The violent electrical storm burst from the heavens over the Jura Mountains. Frankenstein stood at the door of the house, and he watched the storm with delight. Suddenly a stream of fire rose from an old and beautiful oak tree that stood about twenty yards from the house. When the dazzling light vanished, the oak disappeared, and nothing remained but a blasted stump. The bolt of lightning had destroyed the tree—and the power of electricity had gripped Frankenstein's imagination. No more was he interested in alchemy. The theory of electricity and galvanism occupied him—and all the realm of modern science. In his dream, Frankenstein relived the moments of that terrible storm, the bursting thunder and the dazzling light, that was to determine his destiny, that set him on a course from which there was no return.

Next, he saw himself at seventeen. His parents had decided that he should become a student at the University of Ingolstadt, in Germany. His mother died of scarlet fever, and shortly after her death, Frankenstein departed on the coach for the old university town.

How young he was then, how eager to learn everything

there was to know. His professors laughed when Frankenstein mentioned the ancient books of alchemy he had read.

"How useless!" Professor Krempe had cried. "You must
begin your studies all over again."

Frankenstein nodded; he knew the uselessness of those
books as well as the professor did.

Frankenstein studied hard all the branches of modern
science, especially chemistry and physiology. And as he
studied, his mind was filled with one thought, one concep-
tion, one purpose.

"So much has been done!" he exclaimed. "More, far
more, will I achieve. Following in footsteps already marked,
I will pioneer a new way, explore unknown powers, and
unfold to the world the deepest mysteries of creation."

His professors were delighted with Frankenstein's intelligence and interest in his work.

"Continue to work hard," Professor Waldman said, "and
I will have no doubt of your success."

Frankenstein took the professor's advice. For two years
he studied hard, making rapid and brilliant progress, until
in the end he knew as much of the theory and practice of
natural philosophy as the professors of Ingolstadt. He was
about to return home to Geneva when an incident happened that made him stay.

What had interested Frankenstein most was the struc-
ture of the human body and, indeed, anything that was
endowed with life. It was the principle of life, the cause
of generation that he wished to discover, and to learn it, he
studied death. It was a difficult and unpleasant study. Without his extraordinary enthusiasm, it would have been nearly

impossible. But in Frankenstein's education, his father had taken care that his mind should not be impressed with supernatural horrors. He had never been afraid of such things as ghosts and spirits. Darkness had no effect upon his imagination, nor had graveyards or tombs.

He spent days and nights in graveyard vaults, in charnel houses, where the dead are kept. He saw how the form of humanity was degraded and wasted and how the corruption of death succeeded to the bloom of life. He saw how the worm inherited the wonders of the eye and brain.

After he spent weeks examining and analyzing the causes of death, the changes from life to death, a light broke in upon the darkness—a light brilliant and wondrous, yet so simple! He had discovered what no man before him had understood—the secret of life itself! He could scarcely believe that he alone had been chosen to discover so astonishing a secret.

After days and nights of incredible labor and fatigue, he had succeeded in understanding the principle of life. He became capable of bestowing it himself. The discovery was overwhelming. What had been beyond the understanding of the wisest men since the creation of the world was now within Frankenstein's grasp.

Frankenstein stirred in his sleep at the next vision sleep brought. He saw himself alone in the darkest night, in the graveyards near Ingolstadt. It was his work, now that he had the power of giving life, to prepare a body to receive it.

The dissecting room, the slaughterhouse, and the grave furnished his materials. Disturbing the tremendous secrets of the human frame, he worked in his solitary tower chamber, separated from the rest of the house by a long hall and a staircase. In the horrors of his secret toil, he felt he was losing his soul, and he drove himself madly toward the completion of his work. Often his human nature turned with disgust from his workshop of filthy creation, but his purpose—to scale the heights of scientific achievement— spurred him on.

The work was difficult. To prepare a body, with all its intricacies of fibers, muscles, and veins, to implant the organs and connect the arteries, was a labor that nearly defeated Frankenstein again and again. He wondered if he should have started with a simpler being, but his imagination was too exalted. His wish was to give life to a man.

He found, when he had begun the creation of a human being, that the smallness of the parts stopped him from working as quickly as he wished. Contrary to his first intention, therefore, he made the being of a gigantic stature, about eight feet in height and proportionately broad.

Months passed, and in those months, Frankenstein's ambition bore him onward like a hurricane. To break through the boundaries of life and death! To create a new species of beings who would bless him as their creator! He might even, in time, though now he could not, learn enough to bring the dead back to life.

These thoughts supported him during the horror of his labors. He was pale, emaciated from lack of food, often feverish as he pursued Nature to her hiding places.

The graveyard! The vision of that dark, silent place, where only the moon witnessed his unhallowed labor, would not leave Frankenstein's sleeping mind. He watched himself bending over an open grave, the coffin lid gaping to expose the body in its shroud, the graveworms crawling among the folds. He bent closer, in the cold, shadowed night, and thought he saw his mother.

Frankenstein woke from his sleep with horror; a cold perspiration covered his forehead, his teeth chattered, and every limb trembled—and then, by the dim and yellow light of the moon as it forced its way through the shutters, he saw the monster. It moved heavily across the room, coming toward him—the miserable thing he had created.

Frankenstein waited in horror. The monster pushed wider the curtains of the bed. His eyes, if eyes they could be called, were fixed on Frankenstein. The monster's jaws opened, and he muttered some strange, hoarse sounds, while a grin wrinkled his cheeks. He might have spoken, but Frankenstein did not wait to hear. The monster stretched out his hand, seemingly to stop his creator, but Frankenstein escaped, leaping from the bed and rushing downstairs. He hid in the courtyard of the house, listening, fearing that each sound would announce the approach of the demoniacal corpse to which he had so miserably given life.

No mortal could stand the horror of that face. A mummy brought back to life could not be so hideous as that wretch. Frankenstein had gazed upon him while he was unfinished, and he was ugly then. But when those muscles, joints, and face became capable of motion, the awful thing became a creature more nightmarish than any mind could imagine. And its hugeness, the very hugeness Frankenstein had planned, only exaggerated its monstrosity.

In the cold, dark courtyard, Dr. Frankenstein felt his pulse beat so rapidly and violently that he was aware of every artery. Though the storm was over, the stones of the courtyard were chill and damp. Dr. Frankenstein sank down upon them and leaned against the dank, rough wall. He was exhausted from months of labor and the horror of this night. Mingled with the horror, he felt the bitterness of his disappointment. The exalted dreams, the joyous hopes of success in the creation of a noble and rational being, the marvelous sense of his own powers, the worth of his work to science and to humanity—all the heaven of his glorious ambitions now had become a hell to him. The change was so rapid, the overthrow so complete!

Sick with fear, Frankenstein remained in the courtyard throughout the night. Morning came at last, dismal and wet with the rain that poured again from a dark and comfortless sky. His sleepless, aching eyes sought the church of Ingolstadt, with its white steeple and clock. At six, the porter opened the gates of the court, and Frankenstein went out into the streets, pacing them with quick steps, as if by moving quickly he could avoid the monster, whom he feared to see at every turning of the street. He dared not return to the apartment where he lived but felt as if he had to hurry on, though he was drenched by the rain and exhausted in every limb.

He continued walking for a long time, trying to ease the burden of his mind with bodily exercise. Through the narrow cobblestone streets of Ingolstadt he went, past houses whose ancient walls were built so close that they seemed to huddle together for support and warmth. He passed from the old ducal palace, to the Gothic church, to the ruined and crumbling walls of the city. Then, tracing his way back, he was again among the twisting streets. But, though Frankenstein moved on, he walked without any clear idea of where he was or what he was doing. Frightened, he hurried his footsteps, not daring to look about him,

> Like one who, on a lonely road,
>   Doth walk in fear and dread,
> And having once turned round, walks on,
>   And turns no more his head;
> Because he knows a frightful fiend
>   Doth close behind him tread.

The Ancient Mariner—Coleridge

At last Dr. Frankenstein came to the inn where stage-coaches and carriages usually stopped. The horses stamped the cobblestones restlessly, and people were milling about. Frankenstein paused, his eyes fixed on a coach that was coming toward him from the other end of the street. As it drew nearer, he saw that it was the Swiss stagecoach. It stopped just where he was standing, and when the door was opened, he saw within Henry Clerval, his oldest and closest friend, who instantly sprang out.

"My dear Frankenstein!" exclaimed Clerval. "How glad I am to see you! And how wonderful that you should be here just at the moment I arrive!"

Frankenstein all but flung himself upon his friend. He had never been so delighted to see anyone. Being with Clerval again brought back memories of his father, Elizabeth, the scenes of his home. He grasped Clerval's hand and for a moment forgot his horror and misfortune. For the first time in many months, he felt happy. The two friends walked through the town of Ingolstadt toward Frankenstein's college, talking of their friends, of their families, and of Clerval's good news.

"I have finally persuaded my father to let me study here at the University of Ingolstadt with you," said Clerval. "Not natural science, of course. I shall master the literature and the languages of the Orient."

"Nothing could please me more than to have your company," answered Frankenstein, "but tell me again about my father, brothers, and Elizabeth. Are they really well?" It had been more than four years since he had seen them.

"Very well and very happy, but a little worried because they do not hear from you often enough. But, my dear Victor," continued Clerval, stopping short and gazing full in Frankenstein's face, "I have just noticed how ill you look, so thin and pale. You seem as if you have not slept for several nights."

"You're right," answered Frankenstein wearily. "I have been working so hard lately on one particular experiment that I have not allowed myself much rest, as you see. But I hope, I really hope, that the work is now at an end and that I am finally free."

Frankenstein trembled. He couldn't bear to think about, much less discuss, what had happened the night before. He walked more quickly, and they soon arrived at his college. He looked up at the tower, where his apartment was. What if the creature, whom he had left in his rooms, might still be there, alive and walking about? He dreaded to see the monster, but he feared still more that Henry should see him.

21

Frankenstein begged his friend, therefore, to wait a few minutes at the bottom of the stairs while he himself went up to his apartment. He climbed to the topmost landing, passed along the hall, and began slowly to ascend the dark, narrow staircase to the tower. He stood with his hand on the lock of the door and steadied himself. He paused; a cold shuddering came over him. Then he threw the door open forcibly, like a child who expects to find a ghost waiting for him on the other side. But nothing appeared. Fearfully, he stepped in. The room that served as both workshop and sitting room was empty, and even his bedroom was free of the hideous guest. He searched again carefully among the hangings of the great oaken bed; in the cavernous shadows of the open, heavy wardrobe; and then in his workroom, beneath the tables and behind the doors. Books were strewn about, the fragments of a glass bottle lay scattered on the floor, and several garments huddled in a crumpled pile near the wall, as if they had been violently thrown. But if evidence of the room's former occupant abounded, the occupant himself was gone. Frankenstein could hardly believe such good fortune. When he finally convinced himself that his enemy had really fled, he laughed for joy and ran down to Clerval.

They climbed to Frankenstein's rooms together, and a servant soon brought breakfast. Frankenstein was unable to contain himself. It was not only joy that possessed him. His flesh tingled as if it were being pricked by thousands of tiny pins, and his pulse beat rapidly. He could not remain in the same place for a single instant. He jumped over the chairs, clapped his hands, and laughed hysterically.

At first Clerval thought Frankenstein's liveliness was due to the delight of his own arrival. But as he watched Frankenstein more carefully, Clerval saw a wildness that he did not understand in his friend's eyes. He listened to the shrieks of heartless laughter with growing fear and astonishment.

"My dear Victor! What, for God's sake, is the matter?" cried Clerval. "Don't laugh like that! How ill you are! What is the cause of all this?"

"Do not ask me," said Frankenstein, putting his hands over his eyes to shut out the terrible sight. For what he thought he saw, gliding into the room, was the hideous monster, his hands outstretched. "Ask him!" cried Frankenstein, pointing a trembling finger. *"He* can tell. Oh, save me! Save me!" Imagining that the monster had seized him, Frankenstein struggled furiously and fell to the floor.

The Escape   2

IT WAS DIFFICULT for the monster, later on, to remember his own beginning. Like a child's memory of his first few years, the monster's memory of his early weeks was confused. His sensations were so mixed together that he saw, felt, heard, and smelled things all at the same time. He could not tell his senses apart, and he understood nothing of the feelings that seized him as he awoke into the world.

He remembered first the flickering light of the candle. But the small, bright flame was too strong for his eyes. It pressed upon his nerves and forced the monster to close his lids. Darkness then came over him and frightened him. Yet hardly had he felt this before he opened his eyes and the light poured in upon him again. The second time, it was easier to bear.

He found that he could move, sit up, and then stand. With his hands outstretched before him, he stumbled forward and felt his way among the dark, shadowy shapes of things in the gloomy room where he had awakened. Objects fell, startling him with noises. It confused him to be surrounded by things he could touch but, in the darkness, could not see. A dank wind came in through the shutters and gave the monster his first sensation of cold. He stumbled, by chance, upon the open wardrobe and managed to cover himself with some clothes.

It was the gust of air that drew him to the window. He climbed out and moved unsteadily along the balcony until he came to another window, through which he entered. More dark shapes—but from one of them came a sound, a low moan, which the monster sought until he found its origin. Lifting the bed-curtain, he gazed down. Someone on the bed gave a cry. The monster's vocal cords responded with their first sound, and his hand groped instinctively toward the first living creature he had ever seen. The man cried out again and escaped into the darkness. The monster was alone once more.

He lurched from the room, half walked, half fell down the stairs, and found his way into the streets. In the black, rainy night, he wandered along deserted alleys, groping with his hands along the walls as if to find his way out of a maze. When the sky paled into the light of morning, the monster experienced a change in his sensations. In the dark, troublesome objects had surrounded him. Now he found that he could wander easily, with no obstacles that he could not either climb over or avoid. He left the city and wandered into the open country.

If the light had at first pleased him, by noon the heat of the sun wearied him, and the day's brightness after the rain hurt his eyes. His wanderings took him to the forest near Ingolstadt, and he found a place under the trees by the side of a brook. Here he lay and rested until he felt the first torments of hunger and thirst. These roused him from his exhaustion, and he ate some dried berries that he found hanging on the trees and lying on the ground. He satisfied his thirst at the brook and then, lying down, was overcome by sleep.

It was dark when he awoke. He felt cold and frightened in his loneliness. His few clothes were not enough to keep out the dew of night, and he shivered, dimly aware of his own helplessness, his poor wretched misery. Feeling pain invade him from all sides, he sat down and wept.

Soon a gentle light stole over the heavens and gave him a sensation of pleasure. He started up and saw a radiant form rise from among the trees. He did not know it then, but it was the moon, and he gazed at it with wonder. It moved slowly but lighted his path, and he went again in search of berries. He was still cold, but under one of the trees, he found a huge cloak, with which he covered himself, and sat down upon the ground. No clear ideas occupied his confused mind. He felt light and hunger and thirst and darkness. Many sounds rang in his ears, and on all sides, smells greeted his nostrils. The only object that he could distinguish was the bright moon, and he fixed his eyes on it with pleasure.

Days and nights passed before the monster learned to tell his senses apart. Little by little, he saw plainly the clear water that gave him drink and the trees that shaded him with their leaves. He was delighted when he first discovered that the pleasant sounds in his ears came from the small, winged animals that flew about the forest. Sometimes he tried to imitate the pleasant songs of the birds, but he could not. Sometimes he tried to express his feelings in his own way, but the terrible sounds that broke from his throat frightened him into silence again.

The moon disappeared from the night and then came again, while the monster remained in the forest. All his sensations were clear by then, and every day his mind received new ideas. His eyes became accustomed to the light and saw everything in its right form. Now he could tell the insect from the flower and the flowers from one another. He could tell the difference in each bird and the song it sang.

One day, when the winter cold had grown bitter, the monster found a fire that had been left by some wandering beggars. He was delighted by its warmth. In his joy, he put his hand into the burning embers and quickly pulled it out again with a cry of pain. How strange it seemed to him that a thing could bring both pleasure and pain!

He looked carefully at the materials of the fire and was happy to find that they were branches. He quickly collected some, but they were wet and would not burn. He sat rocking himself sadly and watching the fire. As he watched, he saw the wood that he had placed near the embers catch fire. He realized that the heat had dried the branches and, overjoyed by his discovery, busied himself collecting more wood to dry in order to have a large supply of fire. When night came on and the monster grew sleepy, he was worried that his fire might go out. He covered it carefully with dry wood and leaves and placed wet branches upon it. Then he spread his cloak, lay on the ground, and sank into sleep.

When he awoke in the morning, his first thought was of

his fire. He uncovered it, and a gentle breeze quickly fanned the embers into flame. He saw this and made a fan of branches in order to wake the embers whenever he wished. When night came again, he found with pleasure that the fire gave light as well as heat and kept the fearful darkness away.

On another day, when he had been off hunting for berries, he came back to discover some scraps of food left by travelers who had used his fire. The cooked food tasted good to the monster, and he tried, therefore, to cook his food in the same way, by placing it on the live embers. He found that it spoiled the berries but that the nuts and roots tasted much better.

Food became scarce, however, in the wintry forest. The monster often spent a whole day searching, in vain, for a few acorns to stop the pangs of hunger. He decided to leave the forest of Ingolstadt and find a place where his few wants could be more easily satisfied. He was unhappy at leaving his fire, because he did not know how to start a new one. But he was too hungry to stay, so, wrapping himself in his cloak, he struck out across the woods toward the setting sun.

It took the monster three days to find his way out of the forest, but at last he found the open country. Snow had fallen the night before, and the fields were white. The huge expanse of whiteness gave the monster a lonely feeling, and the cold wetness of this strange stuff chilled his feet.

It was early in the morning. The monster longed for food and warmth. Stumbling across the snowy fields, at last he saw a small hut. As he had no memory of the houses at Ingolstadt, he examined the hut curiously. He found the door open, and he walked right in.

An old man was inside, preparing his breakfast. Hearing a noise, he turned.

"No, no!" he screamed as the monster came toward him. "Stay away from me! Whatever you are, stay away!"

The monster shook his head, for he did not understand the words. The man screamed again, ran out of the hut, and sped across the fields.

The monster was puzzled at the man's behavior, but he was delighted with the hut. Here the snow and rain could not reach him. The earth of the floor was dry. And there was food—bread, cheese, milk, and wine. He liked the bread, cheese, and milk, but the wine he did not like at all. After he had eaten, the monster lay down on some straw and fell asleep.

It was noon when he awoke. Lured by the warmth of the sun, which shone brightly on the white ground, the monster determined to travel on. Remembering how hungry he had been, he put the remains of the old man's breakfast into a bag and left the hut.

He walked for several hours across barren country fields. He had learned how to use his body well now, and his stride, if clumsy, was strong and swift.

At sunset, he arrived at a village. How miraculous it appeared to him. The huts, the neat cottages, and the stately houses fascinated him by turns. The vegetables in the gardens and the milk and cheese that he saw placed at the windows of some of the cottages sharpened his appetite.

One small cottage at the edge of the village drew him especially. Its white walls under the low, snug roof reflected the rosiness of the setting sun, and he could see food through its small windowpanes.

The monster crept closer, peered through the window at the family eating supper within, and then opened the door. He had hardly set his foot over the sill when one of the women fell to the floor in a faint and the children began to shriek. Soon the whole village was aroused.

The monster staggered backward, out of the garden and into the lane. Men armed with pitchforks ran toward him; others stopped to pick up heavy stones, which they threw at the monster as hard as they could. The women and children fled, screaming, but the men continued to attack the monster until he escaped, sorely bruised and hurt, to the fields beyond the village.

In pain and misery he ran on until, in the growing darkness, he stumbled upon a low hovel. Fearfully, he crawled inside. For a long time, the monster sat, not daring to move, scarcely daring to breathe lest someone come upon him and hurt him again. He saw that the hovel adjoined a cottage of a neat and pleasant appearance, but after his last horrible experience, he did not dare to enter.

He gazed about his wretched place of refuge. It was made of wood and was so low he could not sit upright in it. No boards, however, had been placed over the earth that formed the floor. But it was dry, and, although the wind entered the hovel through a thousand chinks in its walls, he found that he was at least sheltered from the snow and rain.

Here, then, he stayed, happy to have found a refuge, however miserable, from the terrible weather and, still more, from the cruelty of man.

As soon as morning dawned, the monster crept from his shelter. He wanted to examine the adjoining cottage to see whether he could safely remain in the little hovel he had found. It leaned against the back of the cottage. On one side of the hovel was a pigsty, on the other side, a clear pool of water. The tiny entrance through which the monster had crept the night before was simply a doorless hole. In order to remain there unseen, the monster set to work covering the hole and all the larger chinks with stones and pieces of wood. He arranged the wood and stones hiding the entrance in such a manner that he might move them when he wished to go in or out. All the light he enjoyed came through the pigsty, but it was enough for him.

When the monster had completed the walls to his satisfaction, he carpeted the floor with clean straw. He was by then weak with hunger, too weak to search the nearby woods or fields. On a window ledge of the cottage, he spied a loaf of bread and a cup. While he devoured the bread in large, hungry mouthfuls, the monster turned the cup around and around in his hands. When he had finished eating, he crouched beside the pool of water to drink. He was about to scoop the water with his hands, as always, when he realized for what use the cup was intended. A delighted grin wrinkled his face, and he filled the cup over and over.

Crouched by the water, the monster suddenly raised his head. He saw in the distance the figure of a man and remembered well his treatment of the night before. He clutched the cup and hurriedly clawed at the wood covering up the entrance to his hovel. Once inside, he carefully replaced the wood and twisted himself into as comfortable a position as his cramped dwelling would allow. The floor was at least dry, and because the hovel was built near the chimney of the cottage, the monster felt a little of the chimney's warmth.

Lying there, he decided to stay in this place as long as he could, or at least until something should happen to change his mind. It was a paradise compared to the bleak forest, with its rain-dropping branches and dank earth, where he had spent the first weeks of his life. He finished the last few crumbs of his breakfast and was about to go outside to get a little water when he heard a step.

The monster peered through a crack and saw a young girl with a pail on her head passing before his hovel. Her face, unlike all the human faces he had seen before, was gentle and kind. She was poorly dressed, a coarse blue skirt and a little jacket being all her clothes. Her blond hair was braided. She looked patient yet sad. For a moment, the monster lost sight of her. A little later, she returned, her pail now partly filled with milk. As she walked along, she was met by a young man, who spoke to her in a melancholy voice. He took the pail from her, and they disappeared into the cottage. Soon the monster again caught sight of the young man, now with some tools in his hand, crossing the field behind the cottage. The girl was busy, too, the monster noticed, working sometimes in the yard, sometimes in the house.

The monster wanted very much to see the inside of the cottage. He did not know how it could be managed, until he examined the walls of his dwelling and found that there had once been a window in the wall where now the hovel leaned. The windowpanes had been covered with boards, and in one of these there was a tiny crack. The monster discovered that if he put his eye very close, he could see the room within.

It was a small room, whitewashed and clean but almost bare of furniture. A table, a few chairs, a dresser, a small bed with some extra blankets folded neatly nearby—these were all the cottage contained. In one corner, near a small fire, sat an old man leaning his head on his hands. The young girl was busy arranging the cottage, but soon she sat down beside the old man. The monster watched as the old man picked up an instrument, began to play, and produced sounds sweeter than the voice of the thrush or the nightingale.

The music moved the poor monster to ecstasy, as did the sight of the two beings before him. He thought he had never seen anything so beautiful. The silver hair and the kind face of the old cottager won his reverence, and the gentle loveliness of the girl won his love. As the old man played his sweet, sad music, tears came to the eyes of the girl. This the old man did not notice, until the girl's crying could be heard. Then he spoke to her, and the fair creature, leaving her work, knelt at his feet. He raised her and smiled with such kindness and love that the monster felt sensations of a strange and overpowering nature. They were a mixture of pain and pleasure such as he had never before experienced, from either food or hunger, warmth or cold. He drew back suddenly, unable to bear his emotions.

But he could not keep himself from looking for long. Soon after, the young man returned, carrying on his shoulders a load of wood. The girl met him at the door, helped him to put down the wood, and took some of it into the cottage to place on the fire. Then she and the youth went to a nook of the cottage, and he showed her a large loaf of bread and a piece of cheese. She seemed pleased and went into the garden for some roots and plants, which she prepared to cook.

Soon their dinner was ready, and they sat down to eat. Night quickly fell, but to the monster's extreme wonder, he found that the cottagers had a means of making light last— by the use of candles. He was happy to find that the setting of the sun did not put an end to the pleasure he experienced in watching his human neighbors.

After dinner, the old man again took up the instrument and made more of those wonderful sounds that had enchanted the monster earlier. When the music was over, the young man began to make sounds that did not resemble the songs of birds at all. He was reading aloud from a book, but at that time, the monster knew nothing of words or sentences, and the sounds had no meaning for him at all.

The monster lay back on his straw. How he longed to join these gentle people! But he dared not. He remembered too well how the people of the village had treated him. He would just stay quietly in his hovel, watching, and try to learn all he could about humans and their ways.

Rejection 3

THE MONSTER OBSERVED the cottagers throughout the winter. He saw that they were not entirely happy and that one of the reasons for this was their poverty. They had only the vegetables from their garden, the milk of one cow, and the small wages the young man earned working for a neighboring farmer. The monster noticed that the young people often suffered the pangs of hunger to give their dinner to the old man, who was blind and could not, therefore, see his children's sacrifice.

Their kindness to each other moved the monster. He had been accustomed, during the night, to steal a part of their food for himself. But when he found that in doing this he inflicted pain on the cottagers, he decided to steal no more of their food. From then on, he lived on berries, nuts, and roots, which he gathered from the nearby woods. He also discovered that he could help the cottagers by collecting wood for their fire. This he did by night, after learning to use the young man's woodcutting tools. It pleased the monster that they looked happy and surprised to find the wood piled near the door in the morning.

The monster made two most important discoveries that winter. The first was that these people could express their feelings to each other by making sounds. To the monster, it was a godlike science, and he desired very much to learn it. If only they did not make so many sounds so rapidly! But the monster listened hard, and at last he mastered a few of their words and understood their meaning.

"Fire, milk, bread, wood," he repeated delightedly again and again in his low, hoarse voice. "Felix, Agatha, father, sister, brother." There was another word, "dearest," but he did not understand what it meant.

He learned also about reading . . . that Felix could find the signs for speech on paper. How the monster ached to learn! He wanted so much to make friends with the cottagers, but he knew he had better not try until he had at least mastered their language. Being able to speak to them might make them overlook his ugliness.

Because that was the monster's second discovery that winter—his own ugliness. For months he had admired the perfect forms of his cottagers—their grace, beauty, and marvelous skin. Then, one evening when he was out in the woods, he saw himself clearly reflected in a pool of water. He was terrified of the monster mirrored in the pool. At first he leaped back, frightened at the unknown image. But when he realized that the yellow, wrinkled skin, the black lips, the colorless eyes, the crossing scars—all the sum of those huge, hideous deformities—were indeed himself, he was filled with the bitterest misery and shame. Alas! He still did not know how fatal his ugliness would prove to be.

As the sun became warmer and the light of day longer, the snow vanished, and the pleasant showers of spring brought forth leaves on the trees. The monster continued to observe the cottagers and formed in his imagination a thousand pictures of presenting himself to them. He imagined that they would at first be disgusted, until, by his gentle words and behavior, he should win their favor and afterward their love. He even imagined that it might be in his power to restore happiness to their sad faces. The spring brought him joy. His senses were refreshed by a thousand scents of delight and a thousand sights of beauty. He blotted the past from his memory and gilded his future with bright rays of hope.

It was toward the end of May that an event occurred that changed the monster from what he had been into what he was to become.

A beautiful lady arrived at the cottage on horseback. At the sight of her, the monster noticed, the expression on Felix's face changed from sorrow to radiant happiness and the sadness of the cottagers vanished into joy. The lady, whose name was Safie, was Felix's sweetheart, and the thought that he had lost her forever had been the cause of his sadness.

It was Safie's father who had brought about the cottagers' ruin. The cottagers' name was De Lacey, and Mr. De Lacey had been, only a few months before the monster's arrival, a rich and respected man in Paris. On a visit to Paris, Safie's father, a wealthy Turk, had been unfairly arrested and condemned to death. Felix and his father risked their lives to save him, and Felix fell in love with Safie. But the ingrate had run off, taking Safie, whose hand he had promised to Felix. When the French government found out that the De Laceys had helped the Turk to escape, the De Laceys were exiled to Germany without being allowed to take any of their money with them. Even worse, Felix had lost Safie. Now she had escaped from her father and come to them, and Felix was happy once more.

All this the monster learned later on. But what principally affected him about Safie's arrival was the fact that she could not speak the cottagers' language. The monster watched them use signs at first, and then he understood, because Safie kept repeating certain sounds, that she was trying to learn their language. An idea struck the monster: He could make use of the same lessons!

His summer days were spent in close attention, and it pleased the monster to find that he learned even more quickly than Safie. His speech organs were harsh but supple, and while Safie spoke in broken accents and understood little, the monster understood and could imitate almost every word that was spoken.

Because Felix read often from history books, the monster gained a knowledge of the manners, governments, and religions of the different nations of the earth. He heard about the ancient history of Asia; about the genius of the Grecians; about the wars and virtues of the early Romans; and about the decline of that mighty empire, and the rise of chivalry, Christianity, and kings. He heard of the discovery of America and wept over the fate of the Indians.

These stories gave the monster strange feelings.

"Was man," he thought, "at once so powerful, so grand

and magnificent, yet so cruel and greedy? How can he be at one moment so evil and, at another, so noble and godlike? How can men murder each other, and why is there need for law and government?''

Then, as Felix read on to Safie, the monster learned the strange system of human society. He heard of the division of property, of great wealth and terrible poverty, of rank, family, and noble blood. At length he understood that the possessions most valued by human beings were social position and riches. Without either of these, a man was doomed to waste his powers working for the profit of the chosen few. These words made the monster think of himself.

"And what am I?" he reflected. "I know nothing of my beginning. I have no money, no friends, no kind of property. I have a face and figure hideously deformed and loathsome, and I am not even of the same nature as a man. I am stronger. I can live on coarser food. I can stand heat and cold better than they. I am even much larger than they are. But when I look around, I see and hear of none like me. Am I then a monster, a blot upon the earth, from which all men will flee and which all men will disown?''

These thoughts left him in agony. He tried to dispel them, but sorrow only increased with knowledge. He wished now that he had remained forever in the forest and had learned nothing beyond his first sensations of hunger, thirst, and cold.

"How strange knowledge is," mused the monster. "It clings to the mind like moss on a rock.''

He wished sometimes to shake off all thought and feeling, but he knew there was but one means to overcome the sensation of pain, and that was death—a state that he feared yet did not understand at all. He admired virtue and good feelings and loved the gentle manners of his cottagers, but he was shut out from them. All he could do was watch them, and this increased, rather than satisfied, the desire he had of becoming one among their company. He was alone, a miserable and unhappy wretch.

Other lessons were impressed upon him even more deeply. He heard of the difference between men and women and of the birth and growth of children. He heard how the father protected his children and how all the life and cares of the mother were wrapped up in her family. He learned about brothers and sisters and all the various relationships that bind one human being to another in mutual bonds.

"Yet where are my friends and relations?" whispered the monster to his lonely walls. "No father watched my infant days. No mother blessed me with smiles and caresses —or if she did, I do not remember. My only knowledge of myself is that I have always been, in height and proportion, exactly as I am now. I have never seen a being who resembles me or one who might claim me. What am I?"

He asked the question over and over again and for answer heard only his own hoarse moan.

While the monster improved his speech, he also learned the science of letters as it was taught to Safie. Before long, he knew how to read and even to write, practicing his letters with a stick on the dirt floor of his hovel.

So far, the monster still looked upon crime as a distant evil. Goodness and generosity were always before him in the lives of his protectors, his affectionate name for the

De Laceys. He wanted to be like them.

Then one night, in the beginning of the month of August, the monster was in the woods collecting food for himself and fuel for the cottagers' fire. As he searched about, he came upon a trunk filled with clothes and books. The clothes were even smaller than his own ill-fitting jacket and trousers, and he left them. But the books he seized eagerly and carried off to his hovel.

As he studied the books and pored over their contents, the monster's mind received many new images and greater impressions than before. So far, the cottage of his protectors had been the only school in which he had studied human nature, but these new books developed his mind even more. As he read the histories and the romantic tales, the monster became firm in his admiration of virtue and his hatred of vice.

But one of the books, *Paradise Lost,* excited in him different and far deeper emotions. Reading the story of God warring with His creatures filled the monster with wonder and awe. Then he began to compare his own situation with the characters in the story.

Like Adam, the monster was alone. But with what a difference! Adam had come forth from the hands of God a perfect creature, happy and prosperous, guarded by the special care of his Creator, and allowed to talk with and be guided by his God.

"But I am alone," reflected the monster. "Wretched, helpless, and alone."

Many times he considered himself closer to Satan, for often, like Satan, when he saw the bliss of his protectors, the bitter gall of envy rose within him.

To make matters worse, soon afterward the monster found some papers in the pocket of his jacket, the jacket he had taken the night he left Frankenstein's laboratory. Now he was to discover Dr. Victor Frankenstein!

With trembling hands, the monster clutched the papers and read. They were Frankenstein's journal of the four months that preceded his creation of the monster. In the papers was described every single step in the progress of Frankenstein's work. Everything was written that bore reference to the monster's accursed origin, all the disgusting details of his creation, the minutest description of his odious and loathsome person. All of it was written in language that painted Frankenstein's own horrors of his work, and it was this that stamped forever on the monster a horror of himself.

He sickened as he read. "Hateful day when I received life!" he exclaimed in agony. "Accursed creator! Why did you form a monster so hideous that even *you* turned from me in disgust? God, in pity, made man beautiful, after His own image. But my form is a filthy type of your image, more horrid even for the very resemblance. Satan had his companions, fellow devils, to admire and encourage him. But I am solitary and abhorred."

These were the monster's thoughts in his solitude.

But when he observed the virtues of the cottagers, their generous and kindly habits, he persuaded himself that they would be compassionate about his deformity and love him because he loved them. Could they turn from their door one who, however monstrous, needed so much their compassion, understanding, and friendship?

He waited some months longer, the more to learn and the better to prepare himself. The happiness and the contentment of the cottagers increased. Every day, their feelings grew more serene and peaceful, while the monster's became every day more agitated. Increase of knowledge only revealed to him more clearly what an outcast he was. He cherished hope now and then, it is true, but all he had to do was to see his person reflected in water or his shadow in the moonshine to know that his ever being loved was all a dream.

"There will be no Eve to soothe my sorrows or share my thoughts. I am alone."

He remembered Adam's prayer to his Creator. But where was *his* creator? He had been abandoned, and in the bitterness of his heart, he cursed Frankenstein.

Autumn passed. The monster saw, with dismay and grief, the leaves decay and fall and nature again assume the barren and bleak appearance it had worn when he first saw the woods and the lovely moon one year before. Yet the bleakness of the weather did not bother him. He had found that he was better fitted for the endurance of cold than of heat. But his chief delights were the sight of the flowers, the birds, and all the gay colors of summer. When those deserted the monster, he turned with even more attention to the cottagers. Their happiness was not lessened by the absence of summer. They loved and sympathized with one another, and their joys, depending on one another, were not cut off as the monster's were, by the coming of winter.

The more he saw of them, the greater became his desire

to claim their protection and kindness. His lonely heart yearned to be loved by these kindly creatures. To see their sweet looks directed toward him with affection was all his ambition. He dared not think that they would turn from him with disdain and horror. The poor who stopped at their door were never driven away. He asked, it was true, for greater treasures than a little food or rest. He needed kindness and sympathy. But he did not believe himself utterly unworthy of it.

The winter advanced, and all the monster thought about was his plan of introducing himself into the cottage of his protectors. He pondered different ways, but the plan on which he finally decided was to enter the cottage when the blind old man was alone. He was wise enough to discover that the unnatural hideousness of his person was what had frightened people before, but the old man could not see and so would not be frightened. The monster's voice, although harsh, had nothing terrible in it. He thought, therefore, that if he could just make friends with the father first, the old man might help him gain the friendship of the young people.

One day, when the sun shone cheerfully on the fallen red leaves, Felix, Agatha, and Safie departed on a long country walk, and the old man, on his own desire, was left alone in the cottage. After they had gone, the old man took up his guitar and began to play softly.

The monster's heart beat fast. This was the hour—the moment of trial that would decide his hopes or realize his fears. Save for the music, all was silent in and around the cottage. It was a perfect opportunity, yet when the monster rose, his limbs failed, and he sank to the ground. Again he stood, firmly making himself remove the planks that concealed the entrance to his retreat. The fresh air revived him, and with renewed courage, he went to the door of the cottage and knocked.

"Who is there?" asked the old man. "Come in."

The monster entered. "Pardon me," he said. "I am a traveler in want of a little rest."

"Enter," said Mr. De Lacey. "Sit before the fire. I am sorry that my children are not here. I am blind, you see, and it might be difficult for me to find food for you."

The old man raised his sightless eyes and smiled.

"Do not trouble yourself, kind sir," said the monster. "I have food. It is only warmth and rest that I need."

The old man nodded his welcome. The monster sat down in silence. He did not know what to say next or how to begin his plea. His large hands trembled, and he breathed heavily.

At length, the old man spoke. "By your language, stranger, I suppose you are my countryman. Are you French?"

"No," answered the monster. "But I was educated by a French family and understand that language. I am now going to claim the protection of some friends, whom I sincerely love and who I hope will receive me kindly." The monster paused. "I am an unfortunate and deserted creature. I look around, and I have no relation or friend upon earth. These kind people to whom I go have never seen me and know little of me. I am full of fears, for if I fail there, I am an outcast in the world forever."

"Do not despair. To be friendless is to be unfortunate

indeed. But the hearts of men, unless they are blinded by self-interest, are full of brotherly love and charity. Rely, therefore, on your hopes. If these friends are kind, do not give up hope," said the old man.

"They are kind," answered the monster. "They are the best creatures in the world. But unfortunately, they are prejudiced against me. I have a good disposition. My life has been harmless and even a little helpful. But a fatal prejudice clouds their eyes, and where they ought to see a warm and kindly friend in me, they behold a detestable monster."

"That is indeed unfortunate. But if you are truly blameless, can't you make them see the truth?" the old man asked.

"I am about to try, and that is why I am so frightened," sighed the monster. "I tenderly love these friends. I have, for many months, been doing small kindnesses for them. But they believe I wish to injure them, and that is the prejudice I have to overcome."

"Where do these friends live?" the old man said.

"Near this spot," the monster replied.

The old man paused and then continued. "If you will tell me your whole story and all that troubles you, perhaps I can be of help. I am blind and cannot judge your face, but there is something in your words that persuades me you are sincere. I am poor and an exile, but it will give me great pleasure to be of any service to a human creature."

"Excellent man!" cried the monster. "I thank you and accept your generous offer. You raise me from despair by this kindness. And I hope that, with your aid, I shall not be driven from the society and sympathy of your fellow

46

creatures to dwell alone and friendless.''

"Heaven forbid!" answered the old man. "Even if you were really a criminal, to be driven out could only make you desperate and never virtuous. I also am unfortunate. I and my family have been condemned, although innocent. Judge, therefore, if I do not feel for your misfortunes.''

"How can I thank you, my best and only benefactor!'' exclaimed the monster. "From your lips first have I heard the voice of kindness. I shall be forever grateful. And your kindness gives me hope that the friends I am going to meet will also be kind.''

"May I know the names and address of these friends?'' inquired the old man.

The monster paused. This, he thought, was the moment of decision, which was to rob him of, or give him, happiness forever. He tried hard to answer the old man's question, but he had no strength left to speak. He sank on the chair and sobbed aloud.

At that moment, he heard the steps of his younger protectors. He had not a moment to lose. Seizing the hand of the old man, he cried, "Now is the time! Save and protect me! You and your family are the friends whom I seek. Do not desert me in the hour of trial!''

"Great God!" exclaimed the old man. "Who are you?''

At that instant, the cottage door was opened, and Felix, Safie, and Agatha entered. Their horror and fear flashed before the monster's eyes. Agatha fainted. Safie rushed from the cottage. Felix leaped forward and, with brute force, tore the monster away from his father, to whose knees the monster clung. In a wild fury, Felix dashed the monster to the ground and hit him violently with a stick.

The monster stood up. He could have torn Felix limb from limb, as the lion tears the antelope, but the monster's heart was full of bitter sickness, and he did not touch the young man. He saw Felix on the point of raising the stick again, and, overcome by pain and anguish, the monster ran from the cottage and escaped, unseen, to his hovel.

"Cursed, cursed creator!" moaned the monster.

Why did he live? Why, in that instant, did he not extinguish the spark of existence that his creator had so carelessly bestowed? He did not know. Despair had not yet taken possession of the monster. His feelings were those of rage and revenge. He could have destroyed, with pleasure, the cottage and its people and glutted himself with their shrieks and misery.

When night came, the monster left the hovel and wandered in the woods. Now, no longer restrained by the fear of discovery, he gave vent to his anguish in fearful howlings. He was like a wild beast, destroying objects that got in his way and ranging through the woods as swiftly as a stag. What a miserable night he passed! The cold stars shone in mockery, and the bare trees waved their branches above him. All save him were resting or enjoying themselves. He, like the archfiend, bore a hell within him. Finding himself abandoned, he wished to tear up the trees, to spread havoc and destruction around him, and then to sit down and enjoy the ruin.

But this was too much sensation to last. He grew tired with so much exertion and sank onto the damp grass in the sick powerlessness of despair. There were none in all the world to pity or help him. Should he feel kindness toward his enemies? No.

From that moment, he declared everlasting war against all mankind and, most of all, against the man who had formed him and sent him forth to his misery.

The sun rose. The monster heard the voices of men and realized that it was too late to go back to his hovel that day. He hid in some underbrush and devoted the day to thinking.

The pleasant sunshine and the pure air of the day restored him to some degree of tranquility. He began to believe that maybe what had happened was his own fault. If only he had made friends with the old man slowly. He was a fool for exposing his person to the horror of the young people. They ought to have been warned, prepared for his appearance. Little by little, the monster convinced himself that all was not lost, that he would try again. At night, he crept forth from his hiding place, went in search of food to appease his hunger, and then returned to his hovel. All was at peace, and he waited in silent expectation for the sun to rise and the cottagers to awaken.

The sun rose at last and mounted high in the heavens, but the cottagers did not appear. The monster trembled violently, wondering whether some misfortune had occurred. The inside of the cottage was dark, and he heard no motion. His suspense became an agony.

Later in the day, two countrymen paused beside the cottage. They were soon joined by Felix.

"Must you really move out of the cottage so soon?" asked one of the men. "You will be losing three months' rent and the vegetables in your garden."

"I don't care," replied Felix, while the monster, hiding unseen, strained to catch every word. "We can never live in your cottage again. I have told you what happened. It has made my father very ill, and my wife and sister will never recover from their horror. Take your cottage back with no further discussion and let me fly from this place."

The monster saw Felix and his companions go into the cottage and come out a few minutes later. The monster never saw any of the De Lacey family again.

He stayed in his hovel for the rest of the day in a state of utter and stupefying grief. His protectors had gone and had broken the only link that held him to the world. For the first time, feelings of revenge and hatred filled him without his trying to control them. When he thought of his cottagers—of the mild voice of the old man, the gentle look of Agatha, the beauty of Safie—tears gushed from his eyes. But then, when he reflected that they had spurned and deserted him, anger returned, a wild rage of anger. The horrible scene two days before haunted his vision—the females fleeing, the enraged Felix tearing him from the father's feet.

Furious, the monster, unable to injure anything human, turned his anger toward inanimate objects. As night came, he placed straw and other flammable materials around the cottage. Then he completely destroyed the garden and waited for the moon to sink.

In the night, a fierce wind arose from the woods. The blast tore along like a night avalanche and produced a kind of insanity in the monster's turbulent spirits, which burst all bounds of reason. He lighted a dry branch and danced with fury around the cottage. With a loud scream, he fired the straw and heath and bushes that he had collected. The wind fanned the fire, and the cottage was quickly enveloped by the flames, which clung to it and licked it with their forked and destroying tongues.

When he knew that the cottage was entirely destroyed, the monster screamed once more in agony and hatred and retreated backward to seek refuge in the woods.

Revenge 4

THAT NIGHT and all the next day, the monster spent rampaging through the woods. On the second evening, he sank in exhaustion near the rim of the pool where, months before, he had first seen his own image reflected in the clear water. The late autumn moon rose, and by its light he saw himself again. But this time he knew what he had not known then—the terrible cost of his unnatural appearance.

"I must leave here," thought the monster. "There is too much to remind me of what I have lost."

But to go where? Where, with the whole world before him, should he turn his face? Hated and despised, he knew that every country must be equally horrible. Puzzling the matter over and over, he sat throughout the night, wrapped in his cloak, on the cold, hard ground.

At length, as morning dawned, he thought of Frankenstein. Those papers he had found in the pocket of his jacket had told him that Frankenstein was his creator, his father. And to whom could the monster apply with more fitness than to the one who had given him life?

Among the lessons Felix had given Safie was geography. The monster had learned a little about the locations of the different countries of the earth. In the papers, Geneva was mentioned as the name of Dr. Frankenstein's native town. It was to Geneva that the monster decided to go.

But how was he to direct himself? He knew that he was now in southern Germany and that to reach Geneva he must travel in a southwesterly direction. But the sun was his only guide. He had no compass. He did not know the names of the towns that he was to pass through, nor could he ask information from a single human being. Only from Frankenstein could he hope for help, and toward Frankenstein he felt nothing but hatred.

"Unfeeling, heartless creator!" the monster cried. "You endowed me with perceptions and passions and then cast me out, an object for the scorn and horror of mankind."

But only on Frankenstein had the monster any claim for pity and help, and from him the monster determined to seek the justice he could not hope to find in any other human.

The monster slept that day and began his journey the following night. He knew his travels would be long and his suffering intense as he left the place where he had lived for nearly a year. He traveled mostly at night, afraid to encounter the face of a human being. As he went through the mountains of southern Germany, nature withered around him, and the sun lost its heat. Rain and snow poured down on him, and he saw that the mighty rivers were frozen. The surface of the earth was hard and chill and bare, and he found no shelter. How often did the monster scream curses on the cause of his being! The mildness of his nature had

53

fled, and all within him was turned to gall and bitterness. The nearer his approach to Switzerland and Frankenstein's home, the more deeply did he feel the spirit of revenge kindle in his heart.

Snow fell, and the waters hardened, but the monster did not rest. In a leather wallet lost on a twisting mountain trail, the monster found a map of the country. This, and now and then a sign, helped to direct him, but he often wandered wide from his path. The agony of his feelings left him no peace, and every small incident was food for his rage and misery. There was one incident, especially, that confirmed the bitterness and horror of his feelings.

After four months of painful exposure and near starvation as he traversed the cold German landscape, the monster arrived in the northeast part of Switzerland. The sun had begun to recover its warmth, and the earth to look green. Though he generally only traveled by night, one morning the monster found that his path lay through a deep wood. So dense was the wood that the monster thought he might be able to continue his journey unseen, even after the sun had risen.

The day, which was one of the first of spring, cheered even him by the loveliness of its sunshine and the balminess of its air. Emotions of gentleness and pleasure that had long seemed dead arose within him. Half-surprised by these unexpected feelings, he allowed himself to be carried away by them, and forgetting his solitude and deformity, he dared to be happy. Soft tears again wet his cheeks, and he even raised his eyes with thankfulness toward the blessed sun that bestowed such joy on him.

He continued to wind among the paths of the wood until he came to its edge, which was skirted by a deep and rapid river. Trees bent their branches into the river, and the branches were now budding with the fresh spring. Here the monster paused, not exactly knowing which way to go, and then he heard the sound of voices. Quickly he hid himself under the shade of a cypress. He was scarcely hidden when a little girl came running toward the place where the monster had concealed himself. She was laughing, as if she were being chased in a game. The monster smiled with pleasure at the sight of her with her braids flying as she ran along the steep riverbank.

Suddenly, as the monster watched, the little girl's foot slipped, and she fell into the rapid current of the water. He rushed from his hiding place, plunged into the river, and with a great effort fought his way through the current. He managed to save the little girl and drag her to shore. She was senseless. Gently the monster held her and, not knowing what else to do, sat down with the little girl on his lap and began to pat her cheeks.

In a moment, the underbrush parted, and a man appeared. With a look of horror and disbelief on his face, he dashed forward and tore the little girl from the monster's arms. With staring eyes, he backed away, turned, and began to run into the deeper part of the wood. Without thinking, the monster followed.

"Don't run away," he called out. "You have nothing to fear from me. I did not hurt your daughter. I only pulled her from the river. Please . . . wait—"

The monster's long strides allowed him to catch up with

the man rapidly. As the monster moved forward, his arms outstretched, the man turned, his eyes wild with anger and terror. When the monster drew near, the man aimed a gun that he had been carrying. He pointed the gun at the monster's body and fired. The monster fell to the ground, and the man, with increased swiftness, escaped into the wood.

This, then, was the reward for the monster's benevolence. He had saved a human being from destruction, and in return, he now writhed under the miserable pain of a wound that shattered his flesh and bone.

The feelings of kindness and gentleness that had filled him only a few moments before gave place to hellish rage. The monster gnashed his teeth. Inflamed by pain, he vowed eternal hatred and vengeance to all mankind. Then the agony of his wound overcame him. His pulse weakened, and he fainted.

For some weeks, he led a woeful life in the woods, trying to heal his own wound. The bullet had entered his shoulder, and he did not know whether it had remained there or passed through. At any rate, he had no means of taking the bullet out. His sufferings were increased also by the terrible sense of injustice and by the ingratitude that had caused his pain. His daily vow was of revenge—a deep and deadly revenge, which alone could compensate for the outrages and anguish he had endured.

After several weeks, his wound healed, and he continued his journey. The torment he endured was no longer to be brightened by the warm sun or gentle breezes of spring. All joy was but a mockery that insulted his loneliness and made him feel more painfully that he was not made for enjoyment or pleasure in this cruel world.

It took him two months to cross Switzerland, avoiding as he must the easier, well-traveled roads. Searching his way among the steep Alpine passes, descending into valleys only to climb again, the monster moved on. It was late in the spring when his tortuous journey drew to a close and he reached the outskirts of Geneva.

It was evening when he arrived. He looked immediately for a hiding place in the fields near the town. He wanted to think in what manner he ought to approach Frankenstein. He was tired and hungry and far too unhappy to look with pleasure at the greenness of the fields or the golden sun setting beyond the eastern mountains of Jura. He moved closer to the town and found refuge among some trees in a lovely park just outside the walls of Geneva.

In the soft early evening, the monster fell asleep.

At dusk, a movement in the bushes that encircled the small clearing where the monster slept startled him awake. Before the monster had time to withdraw and hide, a little boy darted into the clearing. He could not have been more than five years old. His sturdy figure was clothed in a blue velvet suit the color of his thickly lashed eyes, and curling hair framed his face, which was rosy with health. The delighted laughter of his game of hide-and-seek dimpled his cheeks. He did not yet see the monster.

As he gazed at the little child, the monster was entranced, and an idea came into his mind.

"Surely this little creature has lived too short a time to have learned a horror for deformity," the monster thought hopefully. "He is too little to mind my ugliness. If I catch him, I can teach him to be my companion and friend. Then I will not be so alone on this peopled earth."

In his need for a friend, the monster crept up behind the child, who was peering out through the bushes. The monster stretched out a large, scarred hand, grabbed the little boy, and spun him around.

When the boy saw the monster's face, the smile froze on his lips, and he covered his terrified eyes with his little hands and screamed.

The monster forced the boy's hands from his eyes and said, "Child, don't scream. Do not cover your eyes. There is no need to be afraid of me. I shall not hurt you. Listen to me."

The boy struggled violently. "Let me go!" he cried. "Let me go, monster! You are ugly; you wish to eat me! You will tear me to pieces; you are an ogre! Let me go, or I'll tell my father!"

The monster held the boy tighter between his hands.

"Boy, you are not going to see your father again," cried the monster. "You must come with me and be my friend now."

The little boy hit the monster with his small fists and continued to scream.

"Ugly monster!" he cried. "Let me go. My father is a very important man. He is Mr. Frankenstein. He will punish you! You do not dare to keep me!"

The monster's black lips parted horribly, drawn back from the ghastly white teeth.

"Frankenstein!" he hissed. "You belong, then, to my enemy—to him toward whom I have sworn everlasting

58

revenge. I shall indeed carry you off, and you shall be my boy, not his!''

The child still struggled in the monster's grasp, twisting and turning and crying out the worst insults he could think of.

"You ugly thing! No boy would want to come with you!" the child shrieked. "You are too horrible for anyone in the whole world to want to be your friend! Ugly, ugly, ugly!" yelled the boy.

The words carried a greater and greater despair to the monster's heart. He could bear them no more. With tears in his eyes, he grasped the child's throat to silence him. In a moment, the boy lay at his feet.

It was an accident. The monster hadn't meant to attack the boy. But as he rose and gazed down upon his victim, the monster felt his heart swell with a hellish triumph. Clapping his hands insanely, he exclaimed, "I, too, can create desolation and despair! My enemy, Dr. Frankenstein, can be hurt as well as I! This accident will bring unhappiness to him, and a thousand other miseries shall torment and destroy him!''

As the monster fixed his eyes on the child, he saw something glittering on his breast. He took it. It was a locket, and inside the locket there was the tiny painting of a very beautiful woman. In spite of the monster's evil mood, the pictured softened and fascinated him. For a few moments, he gazed with delight at her dark eyes fringed by deep lashes and at her lovely lips, but soon the monster's rage returned. He remembered that he was never to be allowed the pleasure of such comely creatures and that, whoever the woman was, she would look at him not with the pleasant expression of the picture but with fear and disgust.

Thinking such thoughts, the monster clenched his teeth in fury.

"Why do I stand here in my agony?" he cried against the darkening sky. "Why do I not rush among mankind and perish in the attempt to destroy them?"

The monster staggered out of the clearing, and from the park, he crossed a country field, seeking a place to hide from his crime.

There was nowhere, nowhere for him to go. Almost out of his mind, he ran madly in circles.

Then, across one of the fields, he saw a barn. As he came closer, he heard no sound. He thought the barn must be empty, so he went inside.

The barn was not empty. As the monster's eyes grew accustomed to the dark, he saw that a young woman was sleeping on some straw. Silently, the monster bent over her in the dark.

The Horrible Truth 5

FOR SEVERAL MONTHS after the monster escaped, Dr. Frankenstein lay ill of a nervous fever. During all that time, Henry Clerval was his only nurse, taking care of him and watching over his friend day and night. Henry did not tell the Frankenstein family how serious Victor's illness was because he knew how the news would worry Victor's father and how unhappy it would make Elizabeth.

Frankenstein was, in reality, very ill. Only such constant care as Henry's could have restored him to health. In Frankenstein's delirium, the form of the monster to whom he had given life was forever before his eyes, and he spoke of the monster feverishly, in the manner of someone crying out in a nightmare. Henry believed Victor's words to be the wanderings of a disturbed imagination, though after a while, he did come to think that his friend's sickness was indeed due to some strange and terrible event.

Slowly and with many relapses, Frankenstein recovered. When he was first able to sit up and look out the window with pleasure, he saw that November's fallen leaves had disappeared and that the green leaves of April were shooting forth from the trees. It was a divine spring, and the season helped greatly in making him better. Little by little, his gloom departed.

"Dear Clerval!" he exclaimed. "How kind, how very good you are to me. You've spent this whole winter, not in study as you promised yourself, but wasting your time in my sickroom. How shall I ever repay you?"

"You will repay me entirely if you get well as speedily as you can," answered Clerval, smiling. "And since you appear in such good spirits, I may speak to you on one subject, may I not?"

Frankenstein trembled. One subject! What could it be? Could he mean the one horrible thing about which Frankenstein did not even dare to think?

"Be calm," said Clerval, who saw Frankenstein grow pale. "I will not mention it if it upsets you. But your father and Elizabeth will be very happy if they receive a letter from you in your own handwriting. They are so worried."

"Is that all, my dear Henry?" Frankenstein smiled. "I shall be only too glad to write a letter to those I love so dearly."

"Then perhaps you will also be glad to read this letter from Elizabeth," said Clerval. "It came some days ago."

"My own dear Elizabeth!" cried Frankenstein, reaching for the letter and opening it.

"MY DEAREST VICTOR:

You have been ill, very ill, and even Henry's kind letters do not reassure me that you are better. One line from you, written in your own hand, is necessary to calm my own and your father's fears for you. If we do not hear from you soon, we shall ourselves come to Ingolstadt. Henry, who has been so good a friend to you, to all of us, writes that you are getting better. We hope with all our hearts that this is true and wait for a letter from you to prove it.

Get well and return to us. You have been away so long, nearly five years. Do return, and you will find a happy, cheerful home and friends who love you dearly. Your father's health is excellent, and he asks only to see you. Ernest is sixteen years old now and wishes for a military career. He is not the brilliant student you are, so perhaps a military career is best for him. I must tell you, too, about our darling little William. I wish you could see him. He is very tall for his age, and when he smiles, two little dimples appear on each cheek. He is so bright, and he charms us all. He has already had one or two little 'wives,' but Louisa Biron is his favorite, a pretty little girl five years old.

Do you remember Justine, the young girl we took into our household, who has always served us so faithfully and who took care of your mother during her last illness? You used to say just one glance from her cheered you. She is so clever and gentle with William, and we love her so much. She sends you her best regards.

Little change, except the growth of our children, has taken place since you left us. The blue lake and the snow-clad mountains never change, or does our contented, happy home. Write, dearest Victor—one line, one word will be a blessing to us. Ten thousand thanks to Henry for his kindness, his affection, and his many letters. We are sincerely grateful. Take care of yourself, I beg you, Victor, and I beg you, write!

ELIZABETH"

"Dear, dear Elizabeth!" exclaimed Frankenstein, when he had read her letter. "I will write her immediately that they need not worry about me anymore."

Less than two weeks later, Frankenstein was able to leave his room. His first duty was to introduce Clerval to the professors of the University of Ingolstadt. In doing this, he suffered badly.

Ever since the fatal night, the end of his labors and the beginning of his misfortunes, he had developed a violent dislike for even the name of natural science. Just the sight of a chemical instrument would renew his nervous symptoms. Henry saw this and removed all Frankenstein's apparatus from view. He changed Frankenstein's apartment, for Henry saw that his good friend hated the room that had been his laboratory. But these cares of Clerval's became useless when Frankenstein visited the professors. When Professor Waldman praised Frankenstein's astonishing progress in the sciences, Frankenstein felt tormented by the reminder of where his work had led him. He writhed under Waldman's words yet dared say nothing. Clerval noticed Frankenstein's pain, but he asked no questions of his friend. Frankenstein was grateful, for though he loved Clerval, he could never bring himself to speak of the horrors of that night.

Professor Krempe's words were even more painful than Professor Waldman's.

"I tell you, Clerval, your friend Frankenstein has out-stripped us all. Stare if you please, but it is nevertheless true. This young man is superior in brilliance to every professor at this university. His future will astound us, I am sure," said Professor Krempe. Noticing that Frankenstein had turned pale, he added, "How modest you are, Frankenstein. You do not like such praise?"

For once Frankenstein was glad that Clerval had never shared his taste for natural science. Henry had come to the university to make himself master of Oriental languages and literature, and Frankenstein, hating his own former studies, now joined Clerval as a fellow student in Persian, Arabic, and Sanskrit.

Summer passed away in these studies, and Frankenstein's return to Geneva was fixed for the end of autumn. But winter and snow arrived too early, the roads were impossible to travel, and his journey was put off until spring. The friends passed the winter cheerfully in Ingolstadt and early in the spring took short trips into the countryside.

"Dear Henry," said Frankenstein gratefully, "you have brought me back to good health and good spirits. Once again I can enjoy the beauty of nature and the excellent conversation of a friend. For too long I selfishly shut myself up for a single purpose, but now I am free from it and shall never think of it again."

"I am glad to see you so happy, Victor," said Henry as they walked in the forest near Ingolstadt. It was the Sunday before Frankenstein's return to Geneva.

It was a glorious spring day. The flowers of the season bloomed in the hedges, the sky was a clear, lovely blue, and

65

the air was fresh and invigorating. Clerval was delighted to see his friend enjoy it all.

In the evening, they returned to their rooms in the highest of spirits. There was a letter from his father waiting for Frankenstein.

"My dear Victor:

You have waited for this note, no doubt, to let you know that we expect you. At first I was only going to write a few lines to welcome you. But that would be a cruel kindness, and I dare not do it. What would be your surprise, my son, when you expected a happy and glad welcome, to see us all in tears and misery? And now, Victor, how can I tell you of our misfortune? How can I give such pain to my long-absent son? I wish to prepare you for the terrible news.

William has been injured—that sweet child, whose smiles delighted and warmed my heart, who was so gentle, yet so gay!

I will tell you now how it happened.

Last Thursday (May 7th), I, Elizabeth, and your two brothers went to walk outside the town in Plainpalais Park. The evening was warm and quiet, and we walked farther than usual. It was already dusk before we thought of returning. Then we discovered that William and Ernest, who had been walking ahead of us, were not to be found. We rested on a bench for a while until they should return. Soon Ernest came and asked if we had seen his brother. He said that he had been playing hide-and-seek with William and that William had run away to hide himself. Ernest had looked for him, could not find him, waited for him. William did not return, though Ernest waited a long time.

Ernest's story worried us, and we continued to search for William until night fell, when Elizabeth suggested that he might have returned to the house. He was not there. We went back to the park with torches, for I could not rest thinking that my sweet boy had lost himself and was exposed to all the damps and dews of night. Elizabeth also suffered extremely. About five in the morning, I discovered my lovely boy, whom the night before I had seen blooming and in active health, stretched on the grass, pale and motionless. The fingerprints of his attacker were plain in the bruises on my boy's throat.

I carried William home. The worry on my face alarmed Elizabeth, and she rushed to see William. She examined him and then his neck and clothes. Finally, she burst into tears and exclaimed, 'Oh, God! It is all my fault!'

She fainted and was restored with extreme difficulty. Then she told me that, before our walk, William had begged and begged her to let him wear a very valuable miniature of your mother that she possessed. The locket is gone and was doubtless what tempted the attacker. We have no trace of him at present, though we make every effort to discover who he was.

William will not, or can not, speak. The doctors say he may be better in time, but as yet the boy can give us no help in discovering the identity of the attacker. He was so badly frightened, poor child.

Come, dear Victor. Only you can console Elizabeth. She weeps constantly and accuses herself unjustly as the sole cause of William's accident. Your dear mother! Alas,

Victor! I now say thank God she did not live to witness this cruel, miserable attack upon her youngest darling!

Come home quickly, Victor. We need your love and consolation. Your affectionate and unhappy father,

ALPHONSE FRANKENSTEIN"

Clerval, who had watched Frankenstein's face as he read the letter, was surprised to see his friend's happy expression turn to despair. Frankenstein threw the letter on the table and covered his face with his hands.

"My dear Frankenstein," said Henry, "are you always to be unhappy? My dear friend, what has happened?"

Frankenstein motioned to Clerval to read the letter.

"What can I say to you, my friend?" cried Clerval. "How awful this is! What do you intend to do?"

"To go instantly to Geneva. Come with me, Henry, to order the horses and carriage," answered Frankenstein.

During their walk, Clerval tried to comfort Frankenstein. He could only express his heartfelt sympathy. "Poor William," he said. "That dear, lovely child. To have been attacked so mercilessly, to feel his attacker's grasp, and now to lie, ill and terrorized, with such a memory to haunt his little mind. Poor little fellow, how dreadful for him. How dreadful for all of you!"

In a daze, Frankenstein thanked Clerval for his sympathetic words. They arrived at the inn, ordered the horses, and Frankenstein bade farewell to his friend.

His journey was very melancholy. At first he wished to hurry on, for he longed to console and sympathize with his loved and sorrowing family. But when he drew near his native town, he slowed his progress. He could hardly bear the strong feelings that crowded into his mind at the sight of so many scenes familiar to his youth. He had been away for nearly six years—two years studying, two years working on his ghastly experiments, half a year ill, and a little more than a year studying with Henry Clerval. Frankenstein wondered how much might have changed in all that time. But more than the wondering made him slow his journey. A sudden fear came over him. He dared not go on. He dreaded—he knew not why—a thousand nameless evils.

He remained for two days at Lausanne, gazing at the serene lake and the snowy mountains. By degrees, the calm and beautiful scene made him feel better, and he continued his journey to Geneva.

The road ran beside Lake Geneva. He could see the black sides of the Jura Mountains and the bright summit of Mont Blanc. He wept like a child.

"Dear mountains! My own beautiful lake! How do you welcome your wanderer? Is your beauty a welcome or a mockery at my unhappiness?"

He was so moved to be back in his beloved native country that he wept again. Yet, as he drew nearer home, grief and fear again overcame him. Night closed around, and the picture of the looming mountains appeared to him a vast and dim scene of evil. He had a feeling that he was destined to be the most wretched of human beings.

It was completely dark when Frankenstein arrived at Geneva. The gates of the town were already shut, and he had to spend the night at a neighboring village. Being unable to rest, he decided to visit the spot where William had been found. As he went, he saw the lightning begin to play on the summit of Mont Blanc. A storm approached rapidly. Frankenstein climbed a hill to watch the progress of the storm.

It advanced. The rain soon began to fall in large drops, and the thunder burst with a terrific crash over his head. The flash of lightning dazzled his eyes, lit up the lake until it appeared like a vast sheet of fire, and then left the world in darkness until it flashed again.

While Frankenstein watched the war in the skies, so beautiful yet so terrifying, he moved on with quick steps. Then, in the gloom, he saw a figure that stole from behind a clump of trees not far away.

Frankenstein stood still, gazing intently. He could not be mistaken! A flash of lightning illuminated the figure and revealed its shape. The gigantic height and the deformity of its face instantly informed Frankenstein that it was the hideous monster to whom he had given life!

"What is he doing here?" Frankenstein wondered. "Could he be"—Frankenstein shuddered—"the one who attacked my brother?"

No sooner did that idea cross his imagination than he became convinced of its truth. His teeth chattered, and he leaned against a tree for support.

The figure passed Frankenstein quickly and was lost in the darkness. Nothing in human shape could have hurt that fair child. *He* was the attacker! Frankenstein could not doubt it. He thought of chasing the demon, but it would have been in vain.

Another flash of lightning revealed the monster clinging

to the rocks of a mountainside impossible for ordinary human beings to climb. The mountain was situated south of the park, and how the monster managed to scale its steep side, Frankenstein could not imagine. The monster soon reached the summit and disappeared.

Frankenstein remained still. The thunder stopped, but the rain continued. All was darkness. The thousand details Frankenstein had tried to forget concerning the creation of the monster now churned in his brain—all the labor beforehand, the moment it had come to life, its escape. Two years had passed since the night the monster came alive. Was this his first crime? Alas! Had Frankenstein turned loose into the world a depraved wretch whose delight was in destruction and misery?

The agony Frankenstein suffered that night cannot be described. Cold and wet, unable to rest, he wandered about in the open air. He thought of the evil being he had cast among mankind, endowed with the will and power to cause horrible suffering, such as the attack upon Frankenstein's own brother. That night, the monster seemed to Frankenstein like his own ghostly vampire, his own spirit let loose from the grave, forced to destroy all that was dear to him.

"God, what have I done?" he wondered. "For what am I responsible?" He shivered in his cloak and stared wildly up at the heavens. For answer, there were only the torrents of rain pouring down from the skies.

Day dawned. Frankenstein bent his steps toward the town. The gates were open, and he hurried through the streets to his father's house. His first thought was to tell what he knew of the attacker and cause instant chase to be made. But he paused when he thought about the story he had to tell.

He had created a being. He had given it life. He had then met this creature at midnight and seen it climb among the precipices of a mountain no one could climb. Who would believe him?

He remembered that everybody knew of his delirium at the time of the monster's creation, and they would believe his tale to be simply a nightmare caused by fever. Would not the story sound like the ravings of insanity? Besides, even if he could make someone believe him, what use would there be in chasing the monster? Who could arrest a creature capable of scaling the overhanging sides of Mont Salève? No. It was better to keep silent, Frankenstein reflected, and he made up his mind to say nothing.

It was about five o'clock in the morning when he entered the large hall of his father's house. He told the servants not to disturb the family and went into the library to wait until they rose. Wearily, Frankenstein threw himself into a chair in front of the fire.

It was Ernest who greeted him first. He had heard Frankenstein arrive and, dressing quickly, hurried downstairs.

"Welcome, my dearest Victor," he said. "Ah, I wish you had come three months ago; then you would have found us all joyful. You come now to share our misery instead. Yet your presence will, I hope, revive our father and comfort Elizabeth. Poor William, our darling and our pride. He still suffers and cannot speak."

A mortal agony crept over Frankenstein. To imagine his family's unhappiness was bad enough. To witness it was even worse, since he knew his own guilt.

"Elizabeth needs comforting most of all," Ernest continued, "since she still accuses herself of having been the cause of William's horrible experience. But since the attacker has been discovered—"

"The attacker discovered! Good God! How can that be? Who could attempt to pursue him? It is impossible. One might as well try to overtake the wind or confine a mountain stream with a straw. I saw him, too. He was free last night," cried Frankenstein.

"I do not know what you mean," replied Ernest, wondering. "But to us, the discovery we have made completes our misery. No one would believe it at first, and even now Elizabeth will not be convinced, in spite of the evidence. Indeed, who would believe that Justine, who was so good, so fond of all the family, could suddenly become capable of so frightful a crime as to attack a defenseless child?"

"Justine! Poor, poor girl! Is she the accused?" exclaimed Frankenstein. "But she is accused wrongfully. Surely, no one believes she is guilty, Ernest."

"No one did at first. But several things have come out that have almost forced us to believe her guilty. And her own behavior has been so confused that it only adds evidence to the facts. But she will be tried in court today, and you will then hear the whole story," answered Ernest.

"Tell me now," pleaded Frankenstein. "I must hear it now."

Ernest sat down near his brother, before the library fireplace. He placed his hand on Frankenstein's arm and began to speak.

"On the morning we found William injured, Justine took sick and was kept in bed for several days. During this time, one of the servants, happening to examine the clothing Justine had worn on the night of the attack, discovered in Justine's pocket the jeweled locket with the picture of our mother in it. The servant, without saying anything to the family, took the locket to the magistrate. Justine was arrested immediately and accused of the attack upon William. The poor girl only confirmed the suspicion by her extreme confusion of manner."

Frankenstein thought this a strange tale, but it did not shake his faith in Justine's innocence. "You are mistaken," Frankenstein told his brother. "I know the attacker. Justine, poor, good Justine, is innocent."

At that instant, Frankenstein heard his father's footsteps in the hall. When his father entered, they greeted each other warmly.

"Father," said Ernest, "Victor says that he knows who attacked William."

"We do, also," replied their father. "Isn't it terrible, Victor, to discover so much criminality and ingratitude in a woman we thought so devoted to us?"

"My dear father!" exclaimed Frankenstein. "Justine has done nothing. She's innocent."

"If she is, God forbid that she should suffer as guilty. She is to be tried today, and I hope, acquitted."

This speech calmed Frankenstein. He was strongly convinced in his own mind that neither Justine nor any other human being was guilty. Thus he had no fear that any evidence existed strong enough to convict her. Frankenstein's story of the monster was not one to announce publicly. Its astounding horror would be looked upon as madness. To believe his story of the monster, people would have to see the creature with their own eyes. If William would speak— But William would not, or could not, tell of what had happened to him. And without William's evidence, there was no use in Frankenstein's telling his story.

The men were soon joined by Elizabeth. Time had changed her since Frankenstein had seen her last. It had endowed her with loveliness even beyond the beauty of her childish years. She welcomed Frankenstein with the greatest affection.

"Your being here, Victor, gives me hope," said Elizabeth softly. "You, perhaps, will find some way to help my poor, innocent Justine. I know she is innocent. She cannot be guilty of such a crime."

"She is innocent," Frankenstein reassured her, "and that much shall be proved. Have no fear."

"Oh, Victor, how glad I am to hear you say so," responded Elizabeth as she took his arm. "Everyone else believes her guilty, and this has made me feel so helpless."

"Dearest Elizabeth, dry your tears," said Frankenstein. "It will all come out right. Now take me to see our little William. How is he today?"

"The doctors hope he will be well in a few months' time," she answered as she led Frankenstein up the wide stairway and along the hall to William's nursery. "But as yet, he is very weak. The poor boy was so terribly frightened, Victor."

Justine's trial began at eleven o'clock that morning. All of Frankenstein's family were required as witnesses, and

Victor Frankenstein accompanied them to court. During the whole, awful mockery of justice, Frankenstein suffered living torture. Were two people, first William and now Justine, to be punished for *his* curiosity in the realms of natural science, *his* unlawful experiments? Was another life to be ruined and *he* the cause? A thousand times would he rather have confessed himself guilty to the crime of which Justine was accused. But he had been absent when it happened, and no one would believe such a confession. He was, therefore, forced to sit by and watch.

Justine seemed to be calm. She looked so honest, so pretty, so innocent. But as the trial began, several strange facts came out that might have staggered anyone who did not know, as Frankenstein did, the truth.

The facts were these: A market woman had seen Justine, early in the morning, near the spot where William was later found. Justine, it was proved, had been out all the night before. When the market woman asked Justine why she was there, Justine appeared confused. When Justine returned to the Frankenstein house and was asked why she had been out all night, she replied that she had been looking for William. Then, when she was shown William's unconscious form, she became hysterical and ill. The locket with the picture was then found in her clothing.

When the court heard these facts, there was a murmur of horror and disgust.

Justine was called on for her defense. She had wept and looked miserable when she was being accused but now did her best to explain the facts.

"God knows how entirely innocent I am," she began. "I

can explain all of these facts if you will listen to me. That evening, I had been given permission by Miss Elizabeth to visit my aunt in a village just outside Geneva. On my return, at about nine o'clock, I met a man who said they were looking for a lost child, little William Frankenstein. I was alarmed and spent several hours looking for William myself. I could not find him and decided to go back to the house. But by then, the gates of Geneva were shut, and I was forced to remain outside. I found a barn just beyond the Plainpalais Park and slept for several hours. In the morning, I searched again, but if I came near the spot where William lay, I did not know it. I recall meeting the market woman, but if I seemed confused, perhaps it was because I was worried and had not had much sleep. That is all I know." Justine paused, then added, "I understand it is the locket that most condemns me, but of that I have no knowledge. I do not know how it came into my pocket. Perhaps the attacker placed it there. But I do not know how. And I do not know why, after he had just stolen it, he should want to part with it so soon. I understand how fatal this fact is for my case, but I beg you, do not let it condemn me. Surely there are witnesses to my good reputation who will tell you that I could never be guilty of such a terrible thing."

Among other witnesses, Elizabeth came forward to defend Justine's character, to speak of her devotion, and to insist upon her innocence.

"Besides," ended Elizabeth, "why should Justine have wanted to steal such a trinket when, because I value her so much, I would have been delighted to give it to her for the asking?"

A murmur of approval followed Elizabeth's simple and powerful appeal. But the approval was not for Justine. It was for Elizabeth's loyalty. The public was still furious at the ingratitude they felt Justine had displayed by her act.

Frankenstein's anguish was now extreme. Was it possible that the monster had not only attacked the child but had also the malice to leave the locket as evidence on the person of Justine? Frankenstein's horror mounted, especially when he saw by the faces of the judges that they had already condemned the unhappy victim. Justine's torture could not equal his own. She knew her own innocence, but Frankenstein suffered the tortures of remorse.

He passed a hideous night. In the morning, he returned to court. His lips and throat were parched. He dared not ask the fatal question. The ballots had all been counted, and he was told the results. Justine was condemned.

With heartsickening despair, Frankenstein then heard that Justine had confessed! What could it mean? Had he gone mad?

Elizabeth was heartbroken when Frankenstein returned home with the news. She wished immediately to visit Justine in the prison to which she had been condemned for life, on charges of attempted murder and theft.

They entered the gloomy prison and went down the dark stairs to the cells below. They saw Justine sitting on some straw in the back of her cell, her head resting on her knees. She rose at seeing her visitors and threw herself at Elizabeth's feet.

"Oh, Justine," wept Elizabeth, "why did you rob me of my belief in your innocence by confessing?"

Justine's voice was broken by sobs. "The priest threatened me that I would go to hell and my soul be damned forever if I did not confess. I did confess so that the priest would bless me, but that confession was a lie. It is the lie that now makes me more miserable than all else. God in heaven, forgive me!" She paused, weeping, and then continued, "Please, sweet lady, do not believe your Justine capable of a crime only the devil would commit!"

"Oh, Justine, forgive my having doubted you," cried Elizabeth. "I shall come here and visit you often, and I shall never give up trying to release you."

"Do not worry about me, dear lady," said Justine softly, her eyes shining. "God is with me now, and, as I think I shall die soon in this place, it will not be long before I shall be with God. May He bless you all. Remember me, dear lady. Do not forget me."

Thus the poor girl tried to comfort herself. But there was no consolation for Victor Frankenstein. He felt himself guilty of the entire tragedy, and a deep and bitter agony filled him as he listened to Justine's farewell.

"Good-bye, sweet lady, dearest Elizabeth, my beloved and only friend. May heaven bless and preserve you. May this be the last misfortune that you will ever suffer. Live and be happy, and make others so."

The next day, as she assuredly wished to, Justine died. Frankenstein entered a hell whose fires nothing could extinguish. From the tortures of his own heart, he turned to see the deep and voiceless grief of his Elizabeth. This also was his doing! And his father's agony over William, this, too! All was the work of his own accursed hands.

Worse, in the deep recesses of his soul, he sensed that this was not the end of their sorrow. He, who would give his life for all of them—he, Frankenstein, who had no joy except through them—would be the cause of yet more tears and suffering.

Torn by remorse, horror, and despair, he saw those he loved watching over the bed of William and the grave of Justine, the first hapless victims of his unhallowed arts.

Face-to-Face 6

NOTHING COULD REMOVE the weight of despair and remorse that pressed on Frankenstein's heart. Justine was dead and at rest, but he was alive to suffer. Sleep fled from his eyes. He wandered about his father's house, feeling like an evil spirit who had committed deeds horrible beyond description. How strange to think that he had begun life with good intentions, that he had thirsted for knowledge to make himself useful to his fellow beings. Now all his youthful hopes were gone, and Frankenstein spent his days brooding under a dark cloud of guilt and self-torture. This state of mind nearly ruined his health again and made all joyful sounds a mockery. Solitude was his only consolation—deep, dark, deathlike solitude.

"You must not sorrow so deeply," said his father. "Too much grief prevents one not only from all enjoyment but even from daily usefulness, without which no man is fit for society."

Yet, his father's words came from a serene and guiltless mind. Such was not Frankenstein's case, and he could only feel despair and hide himself as much as possible from his father's view.

As it was June and the beginning of summer, the family soon left Geneva for their country home at Belrive. This change was especially welcome to Frankenstein. The shutting of the gates regularly at ten o'clock and the impossibility of staying out on the lake after that hour had made living within the walls of Geneva very uncomfortable for him. Now he was free, out in the country, to seek the solitude he so much needed.

Often, after the rest of the family had gone to bed, Frankenstein took a boat out on Lake Geneva and, with sails set, let the wind carry him far out to the middle of the dark waters. There he was alone with his miserable reflections. Often he was tempted, when all was at peace around him and he the only unquiet thing that wandered restless, to plunge into the silent lake and let the waters close over him and his calamities forever. But then he thought of Elizabeth, whom he loved, and his father and brothers. He could not leave them unprotected and exposed to the malice of the fiend whom he had let loose among them.

This was what tortured Frankenstein most. He lived in daily fear that the monster whom he had created would attack again and again, as long as anyone Frankenstein loved remained alive.

Frankenstein's hatred of this fiend cannot be described. When he thought of the monster, he ground his teeth, his eyes became inflamed, and he wished for nothing so much as to see the monster again, in order to avenge the attack on William and the death of Justine.

When he saw Elizabeth bending in care over little William's bed or listened to her mourning the death of Justine, Frankenstein suffered the most agony. It made him feel, though he had not actually committed any, as though he were guilty of a crime.

Neither his father's concern nor Elizabeth's love could help him. Less and less often was he able to find peace. Finally, one day, his whirlwind passions drove him to seek relief in bodily exercise and a change of scene. He hired a horse and rode toward the near Alpine valleys and sought, in the magnificence and the eternity of such scenes, to forget himself and his sorrows.

He decided to travel to the valley of Chamonix, high in the French Alps. It was August, and the weather was lovely as Frankenstein rode up the ravine of the Arve River. The weight upon his spirit lightened as he went higher in the ravine. The immense mountains and cliffs hung over him on each side, and the sound of the river raged among the rocks. Still he made his horse climb higher, and the ravine grew more magnificent than before. Ruined castles hung on the steep precipices of the mountains, and behind these mountains were the mighty Alps. Their white and shining peaks towered above all, as if they belonged to another earth and were the home of another race of beings.

Frankenstein crossed the ravine over the bridge of Pélissier and began to climb the mountain that overhung the ravine. Soon after, he entered the valley of Chamonix. Here were no more ruined castles but only the high and snowy mountains. Immense glaciers approached the road, and he heard the rumbling thunder of a falling avalanche. Glorious and supreme, Mont Blanc raised its domed peak majestically over all.

A tingling, long-lost sense of pleasure came to Frankenstein as he rode toward the village of Chamonix. In his room at the inn, he remained at the window long into the night, watching the lightning play above Mont Blanc and listening to the rushing of the Arve River as it pursued its noisy way beneath. At length the sound soothed him, and sleep came at last.

For a day, Frankenstein rested and roamed about the valley at the foot of the glacier. The steep sides of vast mountains were before him, and the solemn silence was broken only by the thunderous sounds of an avalanche or the cracking of the ice echoing among the mountains. The silence and beauty did not remove his grief, but at least they quieted it and gave him some measure of peace.

In the morning, it was raining, and thick mists hid the summits of the mountains. Despite this, Frankenstein decided to climb the summit of Montanvert to view the tremendous and ever-moving glacier. He wished to go alone, without a guide, as the presence of someone else would destroy the solitary grandeur of the scene.

It was a steep and dangerous climb, and it was nearly noon when Frankenstein arrived at the top. For some time, he sat upon a rock overlooking the sea of ice. Vast mists rose and curled in wreaths about the opposite mountains and drifted across the glacier. After Frankenstein had rested, he went down onto the ice. The surface was very uneven, rising like the waves of a troubled sea. The field of ice was wide, and he spent nearly two hours in crossing it. The opposite mountain was a bare, perpendicular rock. When he reached it, Frankenstein could see Montanvert exactly across from him at a distance of three miles. He remained in a crevice of the rock and gazed at the river of ice as it wound among the mountains, whose icy and glittering peaks shone in the sunlight over the clouds.

"How marvelous!" Frankenstein cried aloud, and as he did, he suddenly saw a figure, at some distance, advancing toward him with superhuman speed. It bounded over the crevices in the ice, among which Frankenstein had walked with caution. Its stature, also, as it approached, seemed to Frankenstein larger than that of a man. Frankenstein was troubled. A mist came over his eyes, and he felt a faintness seize him. But the cold air of the mountains restored him, and he looked again.

It was the monster, the wretch whom he had created! The horrible and loathsome sight made Frankenstein tremble with rage. Standing against the rock, Frankenstein resolved to wait until the monster came near and then to kill him.

The mists parted. The monster came closer. His face spoke bitter anguish, combined with scorn and malice. Its unearthly ugliness made it almost too horrible for human eyes. Under the long cloak, the monster's ragged clothes bared the scarred, wrinkled skin of his throat, forearms, and the huge, dangling wrists and hands.

"Devil!" screamed Frankenstein in raging fury. "How dare you come near me! Are you not afraid of the vengeance I will take upon your miserable head? Begone, vile monster! Or rather, stay, that I may trample you to dust. If only, by killing you, I could bring the victim you attacked back to health—and the one whose death you caused back to life!''

The monster swayed before Frankenstein, the watery eyes fixed on his creator and the black lips curled with defiance.

"I expected this sort of welcome," said the demon. "All men hate the wretched. How then must I be hated, who am miserable beyond all living things! Yet you, my creator, detest me and turn me away. I am your creature. We are bound by ties that can be broken only by the death of one of us. Your purpose is to kill me? How dare you play with life in this way? Do your duty toward me, and I will do mine toward you and the rest of mankind. If you will agree to my conditions, I will leave them and you in peace. But if you refuse, I will feed the maw of death until it is filled with the blood of your remaining friends.''

"Abhorred monster!" cried Frankenstein. "Fiend that you are! The tortures of hell are too small a vengeance for your crimes. Wretched devil! You blame me for your creation. Come on, then, that I may extinguish the spark of life that I so carelessly bestowed.''

Frankenstein's rage was beyond control. He sprang on the monster with all his strength.

The monster easily threw him off and said, "Be calm! I beg you to hear me before you let loose your hatred. Have I not suffered enough, that you wish to add to my misery? Life, though hard, is dear to me, and I will defend myself. Remember, before you attack me, that you made me more powerful than yourself. I am greater in height and strength than you. But I have no wish to set myself against you. I am your creature. You are my lord and king, and I will obey you if only you will do your part and give me what you owe me. Oh, Frankenstein, why are you fair to other beings and trample only me? You ought to give justice, mercy, and affection to me most of all. Remember that I am your creature. I should be your Adam, but instead I am the fallen angel whom you drive from joy. Everywhere on earth I see happiness, which I alone am forbidden. At first I was kindly and good. Misery made me a fiend. Make me happy, and I shall again be virtuous."

But Frankenstein stood firmly on the ice and, raising his arm, pointed his finger toward the distance.

"Begone!" he cried. "I will not hear you. There can be no talk between us. We are enemies. Go! Or let us try our strength in a fight in which one of us must die!"

But the monster did not move and continued to plead with Frankenstein. As the wrinkled black lips formed words, every muscle in the monster's face twitched visibly under the thin, yellow skin.

"How can I make you understand?" the monster cried hoarsely. "Is there no way I can beg for your mercy, no way to implore your goodness and compassion? Believe me, Frankenstein. I was kind. My soul glowed with love and humanity in the first months of my life. But am I not alone, miserably alone? You, my creator, hate me. What hope can I gather from your fellowmen, who owe me nothing? They kick me away, stone me, hate me."

The monster broke off to gesture toward the white and

empty scene. "The lonely mountains and dreary glaciers are my refuge. I have wandered here for many days. The caves of ice, which I alone do not fear, are home to me, the only home that man will allow me. These bleak skies are my comfort, for they are kinder to me than your fellow-men. If the rest of mankind knew of my existence, they would do as you do and arm themselves to destroy me. Shall I not then hate them who hate me? I will not make peace with my enemies. I am miserable, and they shall share my wretchedness."

Now the monster bent closer toward Frankenstein. "Yet, it is in your power to make it up to me and to deliver man-kind from my anger, which will soon grow into so great an evil that not only you and your family but thousands of others shall be swallowed up in the whirlwinds of its rage. Let me make you understand, and do not scorn me. Listen to my tale of what has happened to me. Afterward, abandon me or feel sorry for me, as you think I deserve. But hear me. By human laws, the guilty are allowed to defend them-selves before they are condemned. Listen to me, Franken-stein. You accuse me of murder, and yet you would murder me. But I do not ask you to spare me, only to listen. Then, if you can and if you will, destroy the work of your hands."

Frankenstein shuddered. "Why do you make me remember that I made you, that I am the cause of so much evil? Cursed be the day, abhorred devil, when you first saw light! And cursed be the hands that formed you! You've made me so miserable that I have no power to consider whether I am fair to you or not. Go away! Take from me the sight of your detested form."

The monster raised a huge, hideous hand—not to strike but to place it across Frankenstein's eyes. "Now you cannot see me," said the monster. "But still you can listen to me and grant me your mercy. By the virtues that I once possessed, I demand this from you. Hear my tale. It is long and strange."

Frankenstein flung the monster's hand away in violence and was again seized by a fit of shuddering.

"You are cold," said the monster. "You cannot bear this temperature as well as I. Come to my hut upon the mountain. The sun is still high in the heavens. Before it sets beyond the snowy peaks, you will have heard my story and can decide. It will then rest on you whether I leave mankind forever and lead a harmless life or become a force of evil to terrify you and your fellow beings."

As the monster spoke, he led the way across the ice. Frankenstein followed, partly from curiosity and partly because he had begun to be impressed by the monster's arguments. For the first time, Frankenstein considered the duties of a creator toward his creature and that he ought to make his creature happy before he complained of the creature's wickedness.

He went with his monster, therefore, across the ice, and they climbed the opposite rock. The air was cold, and it started to rain again. The monster climbed quickly and waited for Frankenstein at the door of the hut, with a look of triumph. With a heavy heart, Frankenstein passed before the monster and entered the wooden hut. The monster lighted the fire, and Frankenstein sat near it with his odious companion to listen to his tale.

As he listened, Frankenstein was moved to pity the poor monster. When he spoke of the early days of his life, of his confused memory of only the hurtful light and the chilling cold until his arrival in the forest of Ingolstadt, Frankenstein's anger fled. Then the monster went on to tell his creator of his loneliness and his fear, the gradual discovery of his senses, and the hunger for food that drove him from the forest. The monster's voice broke in anguish as he told Frankenstein of the old man who had run from him, of the villagers who stoned him, and of his arrival at the cottagers' hovel.

"There I discovered greater hungers than that for food," said the monster. "I discovered the hunger of the mind for knowledge and of the heart for love. The first hunger, I was able to satisfy in part. I learned to speak, to read, and to write."

As the monster recounted the whole of his experience with the cottagers, Frankenstein could not help being struck by the creature's great intelligence. Imprisoned in the hideous head was a sensitive and capable intellect. How quickly he had learned!

"But I learned also to love," the monster went on, "and learned to need affection. I cannot describe to you the torments I felt on discovering my loathsome appearance and, from your written notes in my pocket, the disgusting details of my creation. Love and affection? Who in all the world could give me these! But still I hoped," said the monster bitterly. "Still my heart was gentle enough to hope that those kindly people who lived in the cottage would not turn me away."

As the monster went on to describe the agony of his final experiences with the cottagers, tears of bitterness and loss fell from his eyes.

"Afterward, cursing you yet needing you, I traveled to Geneva," said the monster. He told Frankenstein how he had saved the life of the little girl who had fallen into the river and how he had been shot and wounded in return.

Then the monster spoke of William and how the child had struggled, hurling words at him too terrible to hear.

"I grasped his throat to silence him, and in a moment he lay at my feet," said the monster. "It was an accident. I did not mean to hurt the child. But as I gazed at him, I felt triumphant in knowing that this act would bring you pain, that I, too, could torment as I had been tormented. Then, as I fixed my eyes upon the child, I saw the locket and, taking it, examined the picture inside. The loveliness of the woman in the picture only reminded me once more of my own ugly form and the loneliness to which I was condemned. I left William then and hid myself in a barn. There was a woman inside, sleeping on some straw. She was young and beautiful. Here, I thought, is one of those whose heavenly smiles are given to all but me. And then I bent over her and whispered, 'Awake, fair lady, your lover is near—he who would give his life for one look of affection.'

"The sleeper stirred. A thrill of terror ran through me. What if she should really wake and see me and curse me and call me a murderer? I did not know if William were alive or dead. The thought that she might waken and tell of my crime against William maddened me. Not I, I decided, but *she* shall suffer. The murder I may have done she shall pay for because I am deprived of all that she could give me. Having learned from Felix how your human law works, I knew that she would be punished. I bent over her and placed the picture in her pocket. She moved again, and I fled.

"For some days, I haunted the spot where these things had taken place. Sometimes I wished to see you and sometimes wished to kill myself and be rid of my miseries. At last I wandered toward these mountains and have remained here since, burning with a passion that you alone can satisfy."

The monster rose from his seat and lunged toward Frankenstein to grasp his shoulders.

"We will not part," the monster said. "I will not let you leave until you agree to my conditions. I am alone and miserable. Mankind refuses me its company. But if there were someone as deformed and horrible as myself, she would be my friend. My companion must be the same as I and have the same defects. Frankenstein, you must create this being."

The monster finished speaking and fixed his look upon Frankenstein in expectation of a reply. But Frankenstein was still too shocked by the monster's request to answer, so the monster repeated, "You must create a female for me. I want a wife, a friend, to live with. Only you can do this, and I demand it of you as a right that you must not refuse."

The pity with which Frankenstein had listened to the first part of the monster's tale had vanished at its ending. Rage burned within him again.

"I do refuse," Frankenstein replied. "No torture shall

make me create another like yourself. Two such evil creatures as you might destroy the world! You may torture me, but I will never consent."

"You are in the wrong," replied the fiend, returning heavily to his seat. "But instead of threatening you, I will reason with you. I am malicious because I am miserable. Am I not shunned and hated by all men? You, my creator, would tear me to pieces if you could. Remember that and tell me why I should pity man more than he pities me. If any man were kind to me, for that person's sake I would make peace with all men. But humans cannot help but hate me, and as I am proud, I will not simply accept this fate. I will avenge my injuries. If I cannot inspire love, I will cause fear, and toward you, my archenemy—because you created me—I swear unending hatred. I will work at your destruction until I break your heart and make you curse the hour of your birth!"

As he spoke, a fiendish rage wrinkled his face into contortions too horrible for human eyes to behold, but he calmed himself and continued.

"I intended to reason, not to grow angry. It is you who are the cause. I did not ask to be created. You created me, and you must help me now. Since neither you nor any of your fellow beings will be my friend, what I ask of you is surely reasonable and not so much to ask. I want a female creature as hideous as myself. It is not much, but it will make me content. It is true that we shall be monsters, cut off from all the world. But that will only make us love each other more. Our lives will not be happy, but they will be harmless and free of the misery I feel. My creator, make me happy! Let me feel gratitude toward you for one kindly act. Let me see that one man, at least, feels sympathy for me. Do not deny me my request!'' the monster pleaded.

Frankenstein was moved. He shuddered when he thought of the possible results of his consent, but he felt that there was some justice in the monster's argument. His tale and the feelings he now expressed proved him to be a creature of sensitivity. Did Frankenstein not owe his monster whatever happiness was in his power to give?

The monster saw Frankenstein's change of feeling and continued. "If you consent, neither you nor any other human being shall ever see us again. I will go to the vast wilds of South America. My food is not that of man. I do not kill living creatures to satisfy my appetite. Acorns and berries are enough for me. My companion will be of the same nature as myself. We shall make our bed of dried leaves. The sun will shine on us as on men. The picture I present to you is peaceful and human, and you must feel that you could deny me only out of cruelty. Pitiless as you were before, I now see compassion in your eyes. Let me beg you to give me what I want so much.''

"You say that you will leave the places where mankind lives," replied Frankenstein, "to dwell in those wilds where the beasts will be your only companions. How can you, who long for the love and sympathy of man, keep your promise? You will return and again seek their kindness and again be hated. Your evil passions will return, and then there will be two of you to destroy us. I cannot do this. I cannot consent.''

The monster lifted his scarred and hideous hands. "How

changeable your feelings are! A moment ago you were ready to agree. Why do you once again harden your heart against me? I swear to you that, with my companion, I will quit the neighborhood of man and dwell in the most savage of places. My evil passions will have vanished if I have a friend, for she will give me sympathy. My life will pass quietly, and in my dying moments, I shall not curse my maker.''

His words had a strange effect upon Frankenstein. He pitied the monster and felt a wish to make him happy. But when Frankenstein gazed on the monster, when he saw the filthy mass that moved and talked, his heart sickened with horror and hatred. The monster was right. If even his creator could not bear the sight of him, no one could. This being so, Frankenstein felt he had no right to deny the monster the one sort of creature who would keep him company, a hideous living corpse like himself.

''You swear,'' Frankenstein said finally, ''to be harmless. But have you not already done enough evil to make me distrust you? Perhaps your wanting a companion is a trick so that you may have help in your destruction and revenge.''

''Stop playing with me,'' groaned the monster. ''I demand an answer. I have already explained that it is my loneliness that makes me evil. With someone at my side, I shall no longer be alone and shall feel no more of that anger that makes me vengeful. I need only affection, Frankenstein, to make me good.''

Frankenstein paused for some time to think, to consider the monster's argument. He thought of the monster's early virtues and the loathing and scorn that had changed virtue to evil. The monster's power and threats he also considered. A creature who could exist in ice caves and climb impossible cliffs was a being no human could cope with. The monster was a thing to be feared.

Turning to the monster, Frankenstein, therefore, replied, "I consent to your demand if you will really swear to leave Europe and every other place where mankind lives, forever, when I give you a female to accompany you in your exile."

"I swear," cried the monster, "by the sun and by the blue sky of heaven and by the fire of love that burns my heart, that if you grant my prayer, you shall never behold me again. Go to your home and begin your labors. I shall watch over you from afar, but do not be afraid. I will wait until you are ready, and then I shall appear."

Saying this, the monster suddenly left the hut, fearful, perhaps, that Frankenstein might change his mind. Going to the door, Frankenstein watched the monster go down the mountain with greater speed than the flight of an eagle. Soon he was lost from view in the mists that hovered over the sea of ice.

The monster's tale had taken the whole day to tell. The sun was on the edge of the horizon when he left. Frankenstein knew that he ought to hurry down to the valley before darkness, but his heart was heavy and his steps slow. The difficulty of finding firm footing on the steep and twisting paths made his descent even slower, and halfway down, night came upon him. He sat on a rock to rest and watched the clouds pass over the stars. In the strange, silent night,

Frankenstein's thoughts stirred wildly.

"Oh, stars and clouds and winds," he cried out, "you mock me! If you really pity me, crush me now into nothing and put an end to the terrible agony that hangs over my life."

But for answer, there was only silence.

It was morning when Frankenstein reached the village of Chamonix. He took no rest but returned immediately to Belrive. As soon as he entered the country house, he presented himself to the family. They were alarmed at Frankenstein's haggard and wild appearance, but though they questioned him, he made no answer. He felt shut out from their love, from all sympathy, by the horrible task he had to perform. Though he must do it to save them, he felt too loathsome to be in their company. With an agonized look, he left them and shut himself alone in his room.

The Monster's Wife 7

THE MONSTER had been alive for nearly two years now. Days and weeks passed after Dr. Frankenstein's return from Chamonix, and he could not get the thought of the monster or the promise he had made to him out of his mind. Still, Dr. Frankenstein did not have the courage to begin his work. He feared the fiend's revenge, but he could not overcome his loathing for the task he had to perform.

Frankenstein knew that in order to create a wife for the monster, he would have to study again and to reread many books, as well as his own notes. He had heard of some discoveries made by an English philosopher that he thought might be helpful, and he often thought of visiting England to increase his knowledge. But he kept putting the trip off, inventing every excuse he could think of to delay the start of his work. He even began to convince himself that maybe it was not necessary to start to work so quickly.

Then one day, Frankenstein's father called him into the library for a talk.

"I am glad to see your health improving, my son," said

Frankenstein's father. "But you avoid your family, and still you seem to be unhappy. For a long time I have wondered why, but now I have an idea."

Frankenstein gave his father a startled look and turned pale.

But his father continued, "You are unhappy because of Elizabeth, aren't you? You know that I have long wished for you and Elizabeth to marry. You grew up together, studied together, and have always appeared suited to one another. But perhaps you love her only as a sister. Perhaps you are in love with someone else. And I have wondered if the thought of disappointing my hopes for your marriage or hurting Elizabeth's feelings is the cause of your great sadness."

Frankenstein leaned against the fireplace mantle and smiled at his father in relief. His secret was still safe, and he could, at least, make his father happy on the subject of Elizabeth.

"My dear father," Frankenstein said, "I love Elizabeth deeply and tenderly. She is the only woman I have ever wanted to be my wife. Thinking that I should one day marry Elizabeth has been my greatest joy. I cannot imagine life without her."

Frankenstein's father glowed with pleasure.

"You've made me very happy," he said softly. "I know this house has been filled with gloom for these past months, and perhaps that is what makes you gloomy, too. But William is so much better now, and though we can never forget Justine, we must do what we can to create happiness in this house once more. Do you see any reason why you and Elizabeth should not be married immediately? You are young, but as you have your own fortune, I cannot imagine that an early marriage would interfere with any future plans you may have. Don't think I want to tell you what to do, Victor. I only wish to hear, if you will confide in me, how you feel about marrying Elizabeth right away."

Frankenstein listened to his father in silence and for a long time was unable to reply. So many thoughts came rapidly to his mind. Alas! To Frankenstein, the idea of marrying Elizabeth immediately was one of horror and dismay. He was bound by a solemn promise, which he had not yet fulfilled and dared not break—lest his family be stricken with terror! How could he go through the gaities of a wedding with this deadly weight hanging around his neck? He must perform his task and let the monster depart with his mate before he allowed himself the pleasure of marrying Elizabeth.

Frankenstein remembered that he needed the English professor's knowledge and discoveries for his work. He could write letters for the information he needed, but that would be a long and difficult process. It would be easier and more satisfactory to make the journey to England. Besides, Frankenstein could not bear the idea of doing his loathsome work in his father's house. He knew that a thousand fearful accidents might happen that would disclose his horrifying creation. He also knew that he would often lose all self-control and be unable to hide the frightful sensations that overcame him during such hideous tasks. He must leave the people he loved while he did this work. It would not take long. Finishing it would bring peace and happiness. With the promise fulfilled, the monster would depart forever. Or (and this Frankenstein never stopped hoping for) some accident might destroy the monster and put an end to Frankenstein's slavery.

These feelings made him reply to his father, "I would like first to journey to England. After that, Elizabeth and I will be married." Concealing the true reason, Frankenstein gave several excuses for this journey, and his father was content. After such a long period of melancholy, his father thought a pleasure trip might do the young man good.

"Go, then," said his father. "Stay a few months, even a year, and then come back to us happy and refreshed."

There was only one precaution his father and Elizabeth took about Frankenstein's journey. As they were still worried about his health and his dark moods, they wanted Frankenstein to have a companion. They wrote to Henry Clerval. Clerval agreed to join Frankenstein at Strasbourg.

To England, therefore, Frankenstein was bound. As he made arrangements for his journey, one feeling haunted him and made him afraid. During his absence, he would be leaving his family unaware of the existence of their enemy and unprotected from his attacks. Yet, had the monster not promised to follow Frankenstein wherever he went? Might not the fiend accompany him to England, force his presence on Frankenstein now and then to remind him of his promise and to watch over its progress? As awful as this idea was, at least it would mean the safety of his family, and Frankenstein hoped it might be so. Frankenstein's other concern was Clerval. He needed solitude for his work, but for the first part of the journey, at least, it would be good to have Henry's company. Clerval's presence might even keep the monster, as well as Frankenstein's own maddening thoughts, at a distance.

Late in September, Frankenstein left his native country. Elizabeth bade him a tearful farewell as Frankenstein entered the carriage that was to take him away. It was bitter to him to leave, and bitterer still that he should have to pack up once again the chemical instruments he now detested. Filled with dreary imaginings, he rode through beautiful and majestic scenes, seeing nothing and thinking only of the terrible purpose of his trip.

After traveling for some days, he arrived at Strasbourg and waited for Henry Clerval. At last his friend arrived.

"What a difference there is between us!" thought Frankenstein as he greeted his companion. "Henry is alive to the beauty of the world, while I am but a miserable wretch, haunted by a curse that shuts off every path to enjoyment."

The friends traveled by boat down the Rhine River to Rotterdam. It was a lovely voyage, and even Frankenstein took pleasure in the sight of the beautiful ruined castles set on tremendous cliffs, overlooking the dark Rhine. From Rotterdam, they proceeded by sea to England. It was on a clear morning, toward the end of December, that Frankenstein first saw the white cliffs of Britain, and, soon after, there were the steeples of London, with St. Paul's Cathedral towering above all.

The two men determined to spend several months in London, Clerval to enjoy himself and further his project to visit India, and Frankenstein to seek the information necessary for his work. He spent long days and nights discussing various branches of science with England's greatest natural philosophers. He had, besides, the most unpleasant task of all—to collect the materials for his new creation. Again he experienced the horror of gathering bones from charnel houses, disturbing the dead in their graves, choosing the necessary organs from dissecting rooms, and penetrating the secrets of the human frame. It tortured Frankenstein to think for what purpose he packed so carefully all the parts of what was to become his second living corpse.

In March, Frankenstein and Clerval left London to visit some friends at Perth in Scotland. To please Clerval, they made the journey slowly in order to view the lovely countryside and historical places of England. But when the journey came to an end, Frankenstein was not sorry. He had now neglected his promise for a long time, and he feared the results of the demon's disappointment. The monster might have, after all, remained in Switzerland and even now be taking his revenge on Frankenstein's family. Frankenstein waited for their letters with feverish impatience. He was also worried about Henry. If the fiend had followed them, might he not take out his anger in attacking Henry?

Suddenly Frankenstein did not dare put off his work any longer. When they arrived in Perth, Frankenstein said, "Henry, do not ask me why, I beg you, but I must be alone for a short time. You stay here with our friends while I go north through Scotland by myself. I may be gone a month or two, but promise not to follow me or try to stop me. Leave me in peace and solitude for a little while, and when I return, I hope it will be with a lighter heart and a happy mood to match your own."

"Only write to me and let me know that you are all right, and I will do as you ask," replied Henry. "Please don't be gone too long, my friend. I shall miss you."

Having parted from Henry, Frankenstein determined to go to the loneliest spot he could find in Scotland and finish his work in solitude. He was certain, suddenly, that the monster had followed him and would appear to receive his companion when the work was finished.

Frankenstein packed his instruments and the crates with their hideous contents and crossed the northern highlands. He had decided on one of the Orkney Islands, five miles offshore, as the scene of his labors. It was a place fitted for such a work, being hardly more than a rock, whose high sides were continually beaten by the waves. The barren soil scarcely supported the five persons who lived on the island, and in the whole place, there were only three huts. One of these was empty when Frankenstein arrived, and he arranged to rent it.

The hut had only two rooms. It was dirty. Part of the roof had fallen in, the walls were unplastered, and the door was off its hinges. Frankenstein ordered the hut to be repaired and bought some furniture and food, all of which had to be sent for from the mainland. So poor were the islanders that they asked no questions. They received the food and clothes Frankenstein gave them and left him alone. He lived, therefore, ungazed at and unmolested while he began his work.

At first, he worked only in the morning. In the afternoon, he walked on the stony beach of the sea to listen to the waves as they roared and dashed at his feet. It was a monotonous, desolate, and depressing scene.

After he had been on the island some time, however, his routine changed. As he proceeded in his work, it became every day more horrible to him. Sometimes he could not make himself enter his laboratory for several days in a row. At other times, he toiled day and night in order to complete the work. It was, indeed, a filthy process in which he was engaged.

During his first experiment, nearly three years before, a kind of enthusiastic frenzy had blinded him to the horror of what he was doing. But this time, he went to it in cold blood, and his heart often sickened at the work of his hands.

All alone, employed in the most detestable occupation, his nerves grew strained. Every moment, he feared to meet his persecutor. Sometimes he sat with his eyes fixed on the ground, terrified that if he raised them, his glance would meet with the thing he dreaded most to see. But he worked on, and as his creation began to take shape, he began to feel hope. Yet even his hope was mixed with strange forebodings of evil that made him sick inside.

One evening, Frankenstein was in his laboratory. The sun had set, and the moon was just rising above the sea. He paused for a while to decide whether he should leave his labor or work through the night to bring it closer to the end. As he sat, his thoughts were in a turmoil.

"What am I doing?" he asked himself for the thousandth time. "Three years ago, I created a fiend whose cruelty has ruined my life and filled my heart with the bitterest remorse. And now I am about to complete another being whose spirit I know nothing about."

Frankenstein gazed at the huge form stretched before him on the table. It was a creature equally as hideous as the first. It had the same yellow skin, which, though it covered the muscles and arteries beneath, was nevertheless wrinkled. It had the same black, flowing hair, though longer and curled. There were the same large white teeth, the watery eyes, and the straight black lips. The only difference was in the form of the body, which was female instead of male.

"But is that the only difference?" cried Frankenstein in an agony of despair. "My God! She might become ten thousand times more evil than her mate and delight in, for their own sake, murder and destruction. *He* has sworn to leave the neighborhood of man and hide himself in deserts. But she has not. And she, who in all probability will become a thinking, reasoning creature, might refuse to agree to a promise made before her creation."

Frankenstein gazed again at his new creation and shuddered at its ugliness.

"They might even hate each other," he thought. "The monster who lives now already loathes his deformity. Might he not detest such ugliness even more when it comes before his eyes in female form? She might also turn in disgust from him to the superior beauty of man. She might leave him. Then he would again be alone and deserted, even angrier than before, at being left by one of his own kind."

Frankenstein trembled with despair as he then thought about the worst possibility of all.

"Suppose they do leave Europe together and go to the other side of the world. Suppose the opposite feelings occur and they like each other. Great heaven! They would then want children, and a race of devils would be born upon the earth to threaten the very existence of mankind. Do I have any right, in saving my own family, to inflict this curse upon the human race?''

Frankenstein had once been moved by the monster's arguments. He had been struck senseless by his creature's fiendish threats to his family. But now, for the first time, the wickedness of his promise burst upon him. He shuddered to think that future ages might curse him, whose selfishness had not hesitated to buy its own peace at the price, perhaps, of the existence of the entire human race.

Frankenstein shook, and his heart nearly stopped when suddenly, as he looked up, the light of the moon showed the monster at the window. A ghastly grin wrinkled his lips as he gazed on Frankenstein and then on the form stretched upon the laboratory table. He clasped his hands, and his mouth opened as if he were laughing.

Yes, he had followed Frankenstein in his travels. He had moved through forests, hidden himself in caves, and taken refuge on wild, deserted heaths.

"Now," Frankenstein told himself, "he has come to mark my progress and claim the fulfillment of my promise."

As Frankenstein looked at the monster, it seemed to him that the face expressed malice and treachery. Frankenstein thought, with a sensation of madness, how he had promised to create another just the same. He gazed once more in horror at the monster's face pressed against the glass and strode to his worktable.

Trembling with passion, Frankenstein tore to pieces the thing he had created. Frankenstein knew that he was watched as he destroyed the creature upon whom the monster had built his hopes for happiness, and he heard the wretch howl in devilish despair and rage.

Frankenstein left the laboratory and, locking the door, made a solemn vow never to begin such work again. Then, with trembling steps, he went into the next room. He was alone. None were near him to cheer his gloom or comfort his sickening depression and terrible thoughts.

Several hours passed. Frankenstein stood at his window, gazing on the sea. It was almost motionless, for the winds were hushed, and all nature slept under the eye of the quiet moon. Only a few fishing vessels specked the water, and now and then the breeze carried the sound of voices as the fishermen called to one another. All was absolutely silent until he suddenly heard the sound of paddling oars near the shore and someone landing close to the house.

A moment later, the door creaked. Frankenstein tried to call for help, but he was overcome by the sensation of helplessness so often felt in frightful dreams when one cannot fly from danger and remains rooted to the spot.

The door opened, and the wretch appeared.

"You have destroyed the work that you began," he said hoarsely. "Why? Do you dare to break your promise? I have endured misery. I left Switzerland with you. I crept along the shores of the Rhine. I have dwelt many months in the forests of England and on the heaths of Scotland. I have been tired and cold and hungry. Do you dare destroy my hopes?"

"Go away," shouted Frankenstein. "Never will I create another monstrosity such as yourself. Never will I make another as deformed and wicked as you."

"Slave!" spoke the monster. "Before, I reasoned with you. I will not reason again! Remember how powerful I am. You think you are miserable now, but I can make you so miserable that even the light of day will be hateful to you. You are my creator, but I am your master. Obey!"

"Never!" Frankenstein cried. "No matter how great your power is, no threats will ever make me create a companion in evil for you. I cannot loose another demon upon the earth. Go! I will never change my mind."

The monster saw Frankenstein's determination and gnashed his teeth in rage. "Shall each man," he cried, "have a wife and I be alone? I once had feelings of affection, but no more. From now on, your hours will pass in dread and misery, and soon the thing will happen to take your happiness away from you forever. Are you to be happy while I grovel in my wretchedness? You can destroy my other passions, but revenge remains. I may die. But first you, my tyrant and tormentor, shall curse the sun that gazes on your misery. Beware! For I am fearless and therefore powerful. You will repent of your cruelty, Frankenstein, I warn you!"

"Devil, be quiet! Do not poison the air with your malice," said Frankenstein. "I have told you my decision, and I am no coward to bend to your words. Leave me. I shall never change my mind."

The monster raised his huge, scarred hand.

"Very well, I will go," he cried. "But remember, I shall be with you on your wedding night."

Frankenstein leaped forward in an attempt to attack the monster. "Monster!" he exclaimed. "Before you threaten

109

me with death, be sure you are safe yourself!''

But the monster easily got away from Frankenstein and ran out of the house. In a few moments, Frankenstein saw him in his boat, which shot across the waters with an arrowy swiftness and was soon lost amid the waves.

All was again silent. But the monster's words rang in Frankenstein's ears, and he burned with rage. Pacing up and down the room, Frankenstein conjured up a thousand tormenting images. How he wished he could have killed the monster! He shuddered to think who might be the next victim sacrificed to the monster's revenge. Then he thought again of the monster's words: *I shall be with you on your wedding night.*

So that was to be the moment of Frankenstein's death! That was the hour in which he was to die at the monster's hands. Frankenstein had no fear for himself, but he sorrowed for his lovely Elizabeth when she should find her lover dead, snatched from her arms by the monster in his vengeful malice. As Frankenstein thought of Elizabeth's endless grief and sorrow, he vowed not to fall before his enemy without a bitter struggle.

The night passed, and the sun rose from the ocean. Frankenstein's feelings grew calmer as the violence of rage sank low into the depths of despair. He left the house, the horrid scene of the night's conflict, and walked on the beach. He wished he could pass his life on that barren rock, because he knew that his return to the world would mean his own death or the death of those he most loved by a demon whom he himself had created.

Frankenstein walked about the island like a restless

specter. Toward noon, he lay down on the beach and slept. In the evening, when he awoke, he saw a fishing boat land close by, and one of the men brought him a packet of letters. Some were from Geneva. One letter was from Clerval. It said that Henry was soon to leave for India and asked that Frankenstein please join him for his last few days in England. This letter recalled Frankenstein to life, and he decided to leave the island.

Yet before he left, there was a task to perform, the thought of which made him shudder. He must pack up his chemical instruments. To do that, he would have to enter his laboratory again, the scene of his odious work.

The next morning at daybreak, he unlocked the laboratory door. The remains of the half-finished creature, which he had destroyed, lay scattered on the floor. Frankenstein almost felt as if he had mangled the living flesh of a human being. He picked his way carefully through the filthy mess and collected his instruments. Then he reflected that he had better not leave the remains of his work to horrify the islanders. He found a large basket into which he put the pieces of the corpse, together with some heavy stones so that the basket would sink into the sea. Frankenstein carried everything to the beach and sat, cleaning and arranging his instruments, waiting for the night to come.

Between two and three o'clock in the morning, the moon rose. He put his instruments and the basket aboard a small skiff and sailed out about four miles from shore. The scene was perfectly solitary. At one point, a thick cloud hid the moon. Frankenstein took advantage of the moment of darkness to throw the basket into the sea. He listened to the gurgling sound as it sank, and then sailed away.

A few moments later, the sky grew more clouded. The wind, from the northeast, was high, and the waves began to threaten the safety of the skiff. The wind drove him farther and farther from the coast. He tried to change course, but the boat began to fill with water, and he dared not try again. His only choice was to drive before the wind. He had no compass nor any idea where he was going. Was he to sail into the wide Atlantic and be lost?

"In that case, the monster will be cheated of killing me!" he exclaimed. "Will he not then take his revenge on my family? Will he not turn on my friends?"

This thought plunged Frankenstein into a desperate mood. He looked at the heavens, which were covered by clouds that flew before the wind and were then replaced by others, and at the sea, which might well be his grave.

Hours passed. At last the wind died away into a gentle breeze, and the sea became free of breakers. Suddenly he saw a line of high land toward the south. He steered eagerly toward the wild and rocky coast and sailed along it until he found the harbor of a town.

People crowded to stare at him as he arranged his sails, but no one greeted him, and no one offered to help. Hearing them speak English to one another, Frankenstein addressed them in that language.

"My good friends," he said, "will you be so kind as to tell me where I am?"

"You will know that soon enough," said a man. "And you may not like it, either."

Frankenstein was surprised to hear so rude a reply and

to see nothing but anger on the faces of the people gathering around him.

"Why do you answer me so roughly?" he asked. "The English are not inhospitable to strangers."

"I don't know the customs of the English," answered the man, "but here in Ireland, we don't like murderers!"

"I do not understand you," said Frankenstein, moving forward onto the dock.

"You will soon," the man spat. "You will have to come with me to Mr. Kirwin, the magistrate."

"But why?" cried Frankenstein.

"To give an account of the death of a gentleman who was found murdered here last night," said the man.

Frankenstein accompanied the man without protest, knowing perfectly well that he was innocent. Little did he expect the calamity, the horror, that was to overwhelm him.

In the magistrate's office, half a dozen men came forward to give evidence. They had been out fishing. A strong northerly blast made them decide to return to port. In the dark, as they walked along the sands, they had come upon the body of a handsome young man about twenty-five years old. He had apparently been strangled. There were the black marks of fingers on his neck.

Frankenstein barely listened to the first part of the tale, but when the marks of fingers were mentioned, he thought of William and went pale.

Then another fisherman swore he had seen a boat with a single man in it not far from shore—the same boat, he thought, in which Frankenstein had landed.

A woman who lived near the beach testified that the

113

night before, she had seen a man come onto the beach in a boat and then push off again.

The fishermen were agreed that, in all probability, Frankenstein had left the body on the beach and, because of the storm, could not get away from shore. He had beaten about on the sea all night and had, this very morning, been obliged to land again.

Mr. Kirwin, on hearing this evidence, desired that Frankenstein should be taken into the room where the body lay, in order to see what effect it would produce. Frankenstein entered the room and was taken to the coffin, where the corpse lay. As he gazed down, his tongue grew parched with horror, his eyes stared wildly, and he trembled in every limb. What he saw, stretched out lifeless before him, was the body of Henry Clerval!

Frankenstein gasped for breath and threw himself on the body.

"Have my murderous experiments deprived you, also, of life, my dearest Henry?" Frankenstein cried out. "I have already hurt one and destroyed another. Other victims await their destiny. But you, Clerval, my dearest friend—"

Frankenstein could bear the agony no longer, and he was carried out of the room in strong convulsions.

For two months, he lay in a fever, on the point of death, raving about William, Justine, and Clerval. He dreamed he felt the fingers of the monster already grasping his own neck and screamed aloud with agony and terror. He wanted to die, to escape the nightmare of his life.

But Frankenstein was doomed to live, and in two months the fever left him. He awoke surrounded by jailers, turnkeys, bolts, and the bars of a prison. His first thought was of the safety of his family. Was there a new murder for him to lament? Had the monster wreaked more destruction while Frankenstein had been sick?

"Your family is perfectly well," said Mr. Kirwin, visiting Frankenstein in his dungeon. "I found some letters in your pockets while you were ill and wrote to your father. He has come to visit you."

In his father's presence, and after the excellent medical care Mr. Kirwin had provided, Frankenstein soon grew well. But he was sunk in a terrible gloom.

"My poor son," murmured his father. "You traveled to seek happiness, but a terrible fate seems to pursue you."

"Alas, yes, my father," replied Frankenstein. "A cursed destiny hangs over my head, which I must live to fulfill. Otherwise, I would have died over the coffin of my poor friend."

A month later, Frankenstein was tried for the murder of Henry Clerval. It had been discovered, however, that on the night of the murder, Frankenstein was still on the Orkney Islands. He was acquitted and freed immediately from prison.

His father wished him to rest longer, but Frankenstein wanted desperately to get back to Geneva. His own life was poisoned forever, but with his protection, the lives of Elizabeth, Ernest, William, and his father might be saved. He might still find a way to destroy the monster, to end its hideous life and even more hideous soul.

The Doctor's Wedding 8

FRANKENSTEIN AND HIS FATHER left Ireland, traveling without pause until they came to Paris. There Frankenstein, still weak from his illness, had to stop for rest. His father urged him to see people, to enjoy himself, but Frankenstein felt he had no right to share in the delights of his fellow beings. He had unchained an enemy among them, whose joy it was to shed their blood. How people would hate him if they knew of his unhallowed acts and the crimes that had their source in him alone.

"Father, let me be," said Frankenstein. "William, Justine, Henry—all were attacked by my hand."

His father had often heard Frankenstein say this but thought these wild accusations were the result of his son's fever. He therefore asked for no explanation, and Frankenstein gave him none. He continued to maintain silence about the wretch he had created, knowing that the world would consider him mad. Besides, what was the point in bringing deep fear and unnatural horror to his father's gentle heart?

"Please don't say such things again," his father begged. "Your imagination—"

"You think I am mad," cried Frankenstein, "but the sun and the heavens, which have seen my operations, can bear witness that I tell the truth. I am the murderer of those innocent victims. A thousand times would I have shed my own blood, drop by drop, to have saved their lives. But I could not, my father! Indeed, I could not sacrifice the whole human race."

The end of this speech convinced Frankenstein's father that his son was deranged, and he shook his head sadly and changed the subject. He did not let Frankenstein speak of those things again.

As the weeks passed, Frankenstein grew calmer in his manner and less violent in his speech. A few days before they were to leave Paris, he received the following letter from Elizabeth:

"MY DEAR VICTOR:

I am so happy to know that you are as near as Paris and that I may hope to see you soon. I have spent such a miserable winter, worrying about you. It has been a year and a half since you left Geneva, and we have all missed you so much.

I am only worried that the miserable feelings you went away with are still with you now, perhaps even worsened by your misfortunes. I do not like to disturb you when you have so much on your mind, but I feel I must tell you something before we meet again and explain something that may ease you.

117

We both know, Victor, that our marriage has been your parents' favorite plan since our childhood. We were told this when we were young and were taught to look forward to it. We have always been playmates and good friends to each other, but it is possible that this brotherly affection is all you feel toward me. Tell me, dearest Victor, do you not love another woman, and was this the cause of your misery?

You have traveled and been away many years. When you came back from Ingolstadt and I saw you so unhappy, I confess that I thought it was because you loved someone else but did not want to hurt me or your father. But that was false reasoning, my dear friend. You cannot throw away all chance of happiness to do your duty. And it would make me miserable to think you married me simply for the sake of honor.

I confess to you, dear Victor, that I love you with all my heart. I wish only for your happiness. Do not answer this letter if it gives you pain. Only be happy and remember that I am your friend.

ELIZABETH"

The letter revived in Frankenstein's memory what he had not thought of for a while, the threat of the fiend: *I shall be with you on your wedding night.* Such was Frankenstein's death sentence, and on that night, the fiend would kill him, tear him away from the glimpse of happiness that promised partly to console his sufferings. On that night, the monster would end his crimes with Frankenstein's death.

"So be it," thought Frankenstein. "If he wins the struggle, I shall be at peace. If I win, I shall be a free man once more. Either way, his power over me will be at an end.

"Sweet, lovely Elizabeth," thought Frankenstein as he read and reread her letter. Softened feelings of joy stole into Frankenstein's heart, which dared to whisper dreams of love and joy—yet his fate had been decided long ago.

He wondered how quickly they ought to be married. The sooner their marriage, the sooner Frankenstein would die. But if he put the wedding off, the monster might in the meantime find other means to take his revenge. He had vowed to be with Frankenstein on his wedding night, yet he had not waited to shed blood and had killed Henry Clerval. There was no point in delaying. Marrying Elizabeth would make her and his father happy, and Frankenstein was not afraid to die.

He returned with his father to Geneva. Elizabeth was waiting. Frankenstein held out his arms, and Elizabeth flew into them with tears in her eyes.

"How silly of you to think even for a moment that I didn't love you," said Frankenstein. "All the happiness I hope for is centered in you. It is true that I have a secret that makes me miserable. I will tell you about it after we are married. But it has nothing to do with my love for you. Let us be married as soon as possible."

Their marriage was set to take place in ten days. Frankenstein had moments of tranquility, but these were often swept away by memories of what had happened. Memory brought madness, sometimes fits of rage and sometimes the quiet of despair. Elizabeth alone had the power to soothe him and to remind him of the joy they would find in marriage.

If for one instant Frankenstein had thought what might be the hellish intention of his fiendish enemy, he would rather have banished himself forever from his native country and wandered a friendless outcast over the earth than have consented to this marriage. But the monster had blinded Frankenstein to his real intentions in making Victor prepare only for his own death.

As the day fixed for his marriage drew nearer, Frankenstein felt his heart sink within him. But he concealed his feelings as well as he could, in order that his family might be gay and happy at the coming event.

All preparations for the wedding were made. They were to spend their honeymoon on the shores of Lake Como at the Villa Lavenze, which had once belonged to Elizabeth's family and had now been restored to her. In the meantime, Frankenstein took precautions to defend himself, in case the fiend should openly attack him. He carried pistols and a dagger constantly about him and was always on the watch to prevent any trickery. He felt so well prepared that he began to be calm, even to wonder whether the monster's threat was not just a dream. Elizabeth's happiness made him happy, and soon the day came when the marriage was to take place.

The marriage ceremony was performed peacefully in the Frankenstein house. Afterward, there was a large party, but Elizabeth and Frankenstein slipped away and began their journey to Lake Como. It was a beautiful day, with the sun warm and the air clear. As they traveled together, Frankenstein experienced the last moments of happiness of his life. He held Elizabeth's hand, and together they gazed upon the shining, snowy Alps, the mighty Jura Mountains, and the clear waters of the rivers and lakes.

"Be happy, Victor." Elizabeth smiled. "How beautiful the world is!"

Toward sundown, they came to Evian, on the eastern shore of Lake Geneva, where they were to pass their first night before going on to Lake Como. It was eight o'clock when they arrived, and they walked for a short time on the shore of the lake, viewing the lovely scene of water, woods, and mountains in the fading light. The wind, which had fallen in the south, now rose with great violence in the west. The moon had reached its summit in the heavens and was beginning to descend. The clouds swept across the sky, and restless waves whipped across the lake. No sooner had they returned to the inn than a heavy rainstorm began.

Frankenstein had been calm during the day, but now the night and the storm brought a thousand fears to his mind. At every noise, his hand grasped the pistol that was hidden in his pocket. He was terrified, but he resolved not to let his life go without a struggle.

Elizabeth watched him in timid and fearful silence, but after a while she said, "Victor, what is it that worries you so? What do you fear?"

"Hush, hush, my love," Frankenstein replied. "After to-night, all will be well. But this night, I am filled with dread."

Frankenstein spent an hour in this state of mind. Then he thought how terrible it would be for Elizabeth to see the battle he knew was coming, and he begged her to go upstairs to bed.

"I'll come in a little while," he persuaded her. "It won't

be long now, but I must put a demon to rest.''

Elizabeth obeyed him. When she had gone, Frankenstein walked up and down the halls of the inn in an attempt to find his enemy. He looked into every corner that might provide a hiding place but could find no trace of the monster.

He was just beginning to wonder if some fortunate chance had ruined the demon's plans, when suddenly he heard a shrill and dreadful scream. It came from the room in which Elizabeth had gone to bed. As Frankenstein heard the scream, the whole truth rushed into his mind, and for an instant he remained rigid with shock. The scream came again, and he rushed upstairs and into Elizabeth's room.

There she was, motionless, thrown across the bed, her bridal bed, with her head hanging down and her pale face half-covered by her hair. Frankenstein rushed to her and took her in his arms. As he smoothed her hair back, he saw that her eyes were closed and her mouth slightly open, as if she were gasping for air. Her body was cold, and on her neck were the marks, beginning to blacken, of those huge and hideous fingers. He realized at once that Elizabeth was dead.

"Elizabeth," Frankenstein groaned. "Oh, my dearest Elizabeth, what have I done to you?"

While he still bent over Elizabeth in agony, he looked up. The windows of the room had before been darkened, and he felt a kind of panic on seeing the pale yellow light of the moon illuminate the chamber. The shutters had been thrown back, and with a sensation of horror, he saw at the open window a figure—the loathsome, abhorred monster. A grin was on the monster's black, wrinkled lips, and with a fiendish finger, he pointed to the lifeless Elizabeth. Frankenstein rushed toward the window and, drawing out his pistol, fired. But the monster's agility saved him as he leaped from the window and, running with the swiftness of lightning, plunged into the lake.

Elizabeth's screams before, and the sound of the pistol now, brought the inn people to the bedroom door. They knocked to be let in. Frankenstein opened the door and showed the men the spot where the attacker had disappeared. They searched all night, some groups on the water, casting nets, and other searching through the woods and about the countryside. It was hopeless. They found no one.

Bewildered by such horror, Frankenstein's head whirled round, and his steps were like those of a drunken man as he returned to Elizabeth's room. There she lay, his lovely Elizabeth, dead—murdered! Why hadn't Frankenstein guessed whom the monster meant to attack?

"As I destroyed his wife," cried Frankenstein, "so he destroyed mine!"

In an agony of despair, he threw himself on Elizabeth's body and wept. Would his misfortunes never end? The fiend had snatched from him every hope of future happiness. What more could happen!

Yet what of his father, of Ernest, of little William? Would the monster now attack the rest of the family, one by one? Frankenstein had to get back to Geneva. Dashing from the room, he ordered horses and a carriage for the following day.

He arrived in Geneva that night, just before the gates were closed. Frankenstein raced into the house. Ernest still lived. But his father, having received news of Elizabeth's death, could no longer support the horrors of his life. A few hours before Frankenstein's arrival, he had died. The cursed demon had claimed another victim!

Wild with anger, remorse, and grief for his father and Elizabeth, Frankenstein nearly went mad. He was now possessed by a rage so violent, a hatred so intense, that he thought of nothing but to take revenge on the monster, the vile demon who was destroying his family.

This time, however, Frankenstein did not confine himself to useless wishes to punish the monster. He wanted the monster within his grasp. To capture him, Frankenstein knew he would need help. At long last, he decided to do what he had never been able to bring himself to do before —to tell his story publicly and to ask for the help of the police.

Frankenstein went to the magistrate's office. The magistrate, Mr. Zucker, aware of the importance of the Frankenstein family and sympathetic with their recent tragedies, greeted his visitor with courtesy and attention.

"Do sit down, Dr. Frankenstein," said the magistrate. "Only tell me what I can do for you, and I shall be glad to be of assistance."

"Thank you, Mr. Zucker," said Frankenstein. He looked directly at the magistrate's face and said slowly, "I have an accusation to make. I know who is destroying my family. I shall need all the help it is in your authority to give in order to catch him."

"Be assured, sir, that I shall spare no effort to find the attacker," answered the magistrate. "Do sit down, sir."

Frankenstein had been pacing up and down the magistrate's office as he spoke.

"Thank you," said Frankenstein. But he continued, in his agitation, to walk about. "Listen, then, to a story so strange that I hardly dare hope you will believe it. And yet, remember, as I speak, that I have no motive for lying and that I swear everything I am about to tell you is the truth. You will see, I hope, that the story is too connected to be mistaken for a dream."

His decision to pursue his enemy to the death had quieted his agony and enabled him to speak of these matters without raving wildly at every word.

He told the magistrate the history of the past seven and a half years, from the time he had first left Geneva for the University of Ingolstadt to study natural science. He spoke with firmness and precision of his discoveries, his experiments, his incredible creation, and the catastrophes that followed, marking the dates with accuracy and keeping his speech free of curses and raging.

As he spoke, Frankenstein saw that Mr. Zucker appeared, at first, totally disbelieving and then, after a while, attentive and interested. Sometimes Frankenstein saw him shudder with horror, at other times look surprised yet believing.

When Frankenstein had finished his tale, he added, "This is the being whom I accuse and for whose seizure and punishment I call on you to exert your whole power. It is your duty as a magistrate. I believe and hope that your human fears and revulsion will not prevent you from performing your duty."

These words caused a great change in the magistrate's expression. He had listened to Frankenstein's story with that half belief people bring to tales of the supernatural, but when he was called upon to act officially, the whole tide of his disbelief returned.

However, he answered mildly. Pushing back his chair with a sigh and a wave of his hand, Mr. Zucker rose and walked over to the window where Frankenstein stood.

"I would willingly give you help in your pursuit," said the magistrate, "but the creature of whom you speak appears to have powers that make him impossible to catch. Who can follow a creature who can cross a sea of ice at such speeds and live in caves and dens where no man would dare go?" Mr. Zucker shrugged. "Besides, it has been some time since his last crime, and no one knows to what place he may have wandered or what region he may now inhabit."

Frankenstein turned sharply to face the magistrate.

"I do not doubt that he lurks near the spot where I live. But if he has indeed taken refuge in the Alps, he may be hunted like the mountain deer and destroyed as a beast of prey. But I understand your thoughts. You do not believe my story, and you do not intend to pursue my enemy with the punishment that he deserves."

As Frankenstein spoke, rage flashed in his eyes, and he frightened Mr. Zucker.

"You are mistaken," said the magistrate. "I will try, and if it is in my power to seize the monster, be assured that he will suffer punishment for his crimes. But I fear, from what you yourself have said about him, that, no matter how hard we try, we shall never find him. I am afraid, therefore, that you must make up your mind to be disappointed.''

"That cannot be!" cried Frankenstein. "But I see that it does not matter what I say. My revenge does not matter to you. I know that revenge is a vice, but I confess that it has become the devouring and only passion of my soul. My rage is unspeakable when I think that the monster is still alive, that this monster I let loose upon the world still exists. You will not or cannot help me. There is only one thing for me to do—and that is to devote myself, either in life or in death, to his destruction.''

The Genevan magistrate stared at Frankenstein as at a madman. He tried to soothe Frankenstein, as he would a child, and again treated his story as if it were a remembered nightmare.

"You do not understand!" cried Frankenstein in a frenzy. "In your ignorance, you do not even know what you are saying!"

At this, Frankenstein broke from the magistrate's office and ran out of the building, angry and desperate. He would have to think of another way.

Final Revenge

FRANKENSTEIN'S POWERS of reasoning were swallowed up and lost in his fury. Revenge alone gave him strength. It shaped his feelings and allowed him to be calculating and calm, when otherwise madness or death would have been his fate.

His first decision was to leave Geneva forever, or for as long as it took to track the monster down. With his parents both dead and Elizabeth horribly murdered, he left William in Ernest's care. Providing himself with some money, together with a few jewels that had belonged to his mother, Frankenstein departed on his wanderings, which were to cease, if need be, only with his death. Where he was to travel, over what vast portions of the earth, he did not know. He did not care what hardships he would have to endure, what hunger or cold or barbarity he would have to suffer. Revenge would keep him alive. He dared not die and leave his enemy alive.

When Frankenstein left Geneva, he knew his first task was to find some clue by which he could trace the steps of his fiendish creation. But his plans were not yet formed, and he wandered near Geneva for some hours, not knowing what path to follow. As night came, he found himself at the entrance of the cemetery where his mother, his father, Elizabeth, and Justine were buried. He entered it and approached the tomb that marked their graves. Everything was silent, except for the wind in the trees, and the night was nearly dark. The spirits of the dead seemed to flit around and to cast a shadow that he felt but could not see.

His deep grief gave way again to rage and despair. They were dead, and he lived. Their murderer also lived, and to destroy him, Frankenstein had to go on dragging out his weary existence. He knelt on the grass and spoke aloud. "I swear, on your graves, to pursue the demon who caused this misery, until he or I shall die in the conflict. For revenge only will I go on living. And I call on you, spirits of the dead, and on you, spirits of vengeance, to help me and show me the way. Let the accursed and hellish monster drink deep of agony. Let him feel the despair that now torments me!"

As Frankenstein's voice rose, he felt the furies possess him and the spirits of the dead surround him and approve his words. He went on speaking until rage choked his throat.

He was answered, in the stillness of the night, by a loud and fiendish laugh. It rang in his ears long and heavily. The mountains echoed the sound, and Frankenstein felt as if all hell surrounded him with mockery and laughter. As the hideous noise died away, a well-known and abhorred voice, apparently close to his ear, spoke to him in a whisper. "I

129

am satisfied," said the voice. "You have decided to go on living, and I am satisfied."

Frankenstein ran toward the spot where the sound came from, but the devil escaped Frankenstein's grasp. Suddenly the moon arose and shone full upon the ghastly and distorted shape as it fled with more than human speed. For just a moment, the monster paused and made a motion with his arm, as if to beckon his creator onward. Then he fled once more across the fields.

Frankenstein pursued him. He followed any clue he could find. Often the clues were false, and he lost many days in searching vainly along the windings of the Rhone River. One day, the blue Mediterranean Sea appeared before him, and by a strange chance, he saw the fiend hide himself in a ship bound for the Black Sea. Frankenstein got on the same ship, but the monster escaped; Frankenstein did not know how.

Through the Ukraine and north into the wilds of Russia, Frankenstein followed in the monster's tracks. Sometimes villagers who had been scared by this horrid apparition informed Frankenstein of the monster's path. Sometimes the monster himself, wanting Frankenstein to follow him, left some clue to guide his creator.

Soon it was winter. When the snows came, Frankenstein was able to see the monster's huge footprints on the white plain. The young doctor suffered terribly from cold and hunger. Once in a while, the country people fed him, but mostly he lived by hunting wild animals that crossed his path and drinking the rain that fell from the sky.

Frankenstein followed, when he could, the courses of

the rivers. But the demon generally avoided rivers because too many people lived along their banks. He therefore forced his pursuer deep into the wilds, the desert places, and the forests. Often, Frankenstein came close to exhaustion, starvation, and death, but these were nothing compared to the torture of knowing that the monster was still alive.

Only in sleep did Frankenstein find peace. When he slept, he dreamed that Henry and Elizabeth had never been killed and that Justine and his father were still alive. When he dreamed, he heard their voices, as happy as they had been long ago. When he woke, his desire for revenge became fiercer still.

What the monster's feelings were, Frankenstein did not know. Sometimes the monster left messages, written on the bark of trees or cut in stone, to guide his pursuer and make him even more furious.

"My reign is not yet over," said one message. "You live, and my power is complete. Follow me. I seek the everlasting ices of the north, where you will feel the misery of the cold and frost that do not bother me. You will find near here a dead rabbit. Eat it and grow strong. Come on, my enemy. We have yet to fight for our lives, but you will still have to go through many miserable hours until that moment arrives."

Jeering devil! Again Frankenstein vowed vengeance and promised the miserable fiend a tortured death.

As Frankenstein went northward, the snows thickened, and the cold grew almost too terrible to bear. The rivers were covered with ice; food was nearly impossible to find.

The triumph of Frankenstein's enemy increased with these hardships. He left another message for his follower.

"Prepare! Your toils only begin. Wrap yourself in furs and buy food, for we shall soon enter upon a journey where your sufferings will satisfy my everlasting hatred."

These words only served to increase Frankenstein's courage and fury. He resolved not to fail and continued to cross immense frozen deserts until, not far from the port of Archangel, he saw at a distance the frozen White Sea.

Frankenstein had been traveling, for the past few weeks, by dogsled, which had allowed him to go so much faster that he had begun to gain on the monster. Now the fiend was only one day's journey ahead of him, and he hoped to catch up before the monster should reach the shore. With new courage, therefore, Frankenstein pressed on and in two days arrived at a wretched village at the sea's edge. He asked the villagers about the fiend and received accurate information.

A gigantic monster, they said, had arrived the night before, armed with a gun and many pistols, and had frightened away the people who lived in one of the cottages. He had carried off their winter store of food and placed the food on a sled. He had then seized many of the village's trained dogs, harnessed them, and driven off across the frozen sea. The villagers thought the monster would soon be destroyed by the breaking of the ice or frozen by the eternal frosts.

On hearing this, Frankenstein nearly despaired. The monster had escaped him. He must now begin a destructive and almost endless journey across the mountainous ices of the ocean—in cold that few humans could stand for long. Yet the thought that the fiend should live and be triumphant made Frankenstein's rage return, and he prepared to follow the monster once more.

He exchanged his land sled for one made to travel the frozen oceans, and he bought dogs to pull the sled and food to carry with him. Then he departed from the land to cross the White Sea and Barents Sea, to reach at last the Arctic Ocean. He could scarcely tell how many days passed as he crossed the immense whiteness. Huge and rugged mountains of ice often barred his passage, and he heard the thunder of the ground sea that threatened his destruction, should the ice break up. But again the ice refroze and made the paths of the sea safe.

He could tell from the amount of food left that about three weeks had passed. Struggling over the top of a sloping ice mountain, Frankenstein suddenly saw a dark speck on the white plain ahead. He strained his sight to discover what it could be and uttered a wild cry when he saw the outline of a sled and the deformed proportions of a well-known form. There was no time to delay! He fed the dogs to give them strength and raced after the speck in the distance. The sled was still visible. Frankenstein did not lose sight of it except now and then when some ice rock hid it momentarily from view. So quickly did he gain on the monster's sled that, after two days, he saw his enemy at no more than a mile's distance.

But then, when the monster seemed almost within Frankenstein's grasp, he suddenly lost all trace of him. A ground sea was heard. The thunder of its progress, as the water rolled and swelled beneath him, became every moment more terrible. He pressed on, but it was no use. The wind rose. The sea roared. With the mighty shock of an earthquake, the ice split, cracking with a tremendous sound. In a few minutes, a wild sea rolled between Frankenstein and his enemy, and Frankenstein was left drifting on a piece of ice that was growing smaller all the time. Soon he must be prepared for a hideous death.

A few hours passed. Several of the dogs died. Frankenstein himself was on the brink of total collapse when, not far off, he saw an unbelievable sight. It was a ship. He had never known of a vessel to come so far north, and the sight astounded him. Quickly he destroyed part of his sled to make oars and began to move his ice raft in the direction of the ship.

The ship's captain had his men pull Frankenstein on board. He was more dead than alive, but after a week under the captain's care, he had recovered enough to talk.

"Are you going north?" Frankenstein asked.

"Yes," replied the captain. "I am making a scientific voyage to the North Pole." The captain stared at Frankenstein, noting the wild expression in his guest's eyes, the suffering so evident on his face and in his thin and feverish body. He felt sorry for Frankenstein and wished to know if he could be of any help. "Why did you come so far on the ice?" the captain asked.

"I am searching for someone who has run away from me," Frankenstein answered.

"Did the man you pursue travel on a dogsled?" asked the captain.

"Yes!"

"Then I think we have seen him," the captain said. "The day we picked you up, we saw some dogs pulling a sled with a huge man in it across the ice."

At this, Frankenstein grew excited and questioned the captain more closely.

"Do you think the breaking up of the ice might have destroyed the sled?" Frankenstein asked.

"It is possible," the captain replied. "But the ice did not finish breaking up until midnight, and the traveler might have reached a place of safety by then."

"I must remain on deck to watch," said Frankenstein wildly.

"Please," begged the captain kindly, "please rest. You are still so weak. I will have one of my men watch for you. Allow me to introduce myself. My name is Captain Walton."

"I am Dr. Frankenstein, and I thank you for your kindness," Frankenstein replied. "Why are you making this difficult voyage, sir?" he asked as the captain led him back to his cabin.

"Since my boyhood," answered Captain Walton, "I have wanted, more than anything else in the world, to discover new knowledge about the earth, particularly in these northern reaches."

A groan burst from Frankenstein. "Unhappy man!" he cried. "Do you share my madness for discovery, then? Let me tell you my own tale, and you will give up the search for knowledge and wisdom and understand the danger of meddling in things better left alone."

"I can see by the grief in your eyes that you have suffered terrible misfortunes," said Captain Walton. "I sympathize and would like to help you if I can."

"Thank you for your sympathy," responded Frankenstein, "but it is useless. My fate is nearly fulfilled. I wait for only one thing, and then I shall be at peace. If you like, I will tell you my history, and then you will understand."

Captain Walton listened, horrified and appalled, to Frankenstein's story. When the doctor had finished, Captain Walton offered Frankenstein his hand and, once again, his help.

"The only help for me," said Frankenstein, "is the death of the monster. He must not live to add to the list of his dark crimes. If I should die and you should ever see him, kill him if you can. Do not listen to him, for he is very persuasive. Once his words had power over even my heart. But do not trust him. His soul is as hellish as his form, full of treachery and fiendish malice."

"I believe your story and will do all within my power," answered Captain Walton.

"And do you now understand the danger of high ambitions in the realms of undiscovered knowledge?" added Frankenstein. "My thoughts and imagination went as high as the heavens, and now I am chained in an eternal hell. Once I exulted in my powers to be useful to humanity, but I failed, and my life has been ruined by my mad scheme."

It was now September. Frankenstein had been on board the ship for a month, growing weaker and more feverish each day. The ice, which had never broken up enough for the ship to move on, began to thicken and close about the ship, until it was in danger of being crushed. The cold was terrible, and the crew was frightened.

In the middle of the month, the ice began to move again, and roarings like thunder were heard at a distance as the islands split and cracked. Soon the ice near the ship cracked, and huge ice floes were driven north, leaving a clear passage to the south. The sailors begged Captain Walton not to go farther north but to return to England. Captain Walton was forced to consent.

"You go," said Frankenstein when he heard this, "but I cannot. In a fit of enthusiastic madness, I created a rational creature to whom I owed happiness and well-being. But I could not give him that happiness without endangering my own species, to whom I owe an even greater duty. In return for my refusing to create a wife for him, the monster destroyed my family and friends. Miserable himself, he devotes his life to making others miserable. He must be destroyed, and I must destroy him."

"But you cannot remain behind, and I must sail in the morning," said the captain.

"I must remain here, and I will," said Frankenstein firmly. He went out on deck to spend his last night on board, watching.

"We will take turns," said the captain, noting how pale and ill Frankenstein looked. "You go below and rest for a few hours, and later on I will wake you."

Frankenstein nodded and returned to the cabin. The captain kept watch for an hour, and then he heard a strange and unusual sound. It was coming from below, from the cabin where Frankenstein slept. The captain dashed below decks and flung open the cabin door. His jaw dropped in horror.

He saw immediately that Frankenstein was dead—whether from the feverish illness he suffered or from shock, the captain never knew. Over the dead Frankenstein loomed a gigantic figure, deformed and hideous. As he bent over Frankenstein, long locks of ragged hair hid his face from the captain's view, but one vast hand was stretched out. To the captain, the hand appeared like that of a mummy. At the sound of the captain's entrance, the monster turned quickly around. Never had the captain seen anything so horrible as that face, hideous to begin with and now distorted even more by a strange combination of rage and sorrow.

"That is also my victim," the monster whispered hoarsely, pointing at Frankenstein. "Now that he is dead, my crimes are complete. Ah, Frankenstein. What use is it now that I ask your pardon—I who, in destroying all you loved, destroyed you! Alas, he is cold—he cannot answer me."

The captain thought of his promise to Frankenstein to kill the monster if he appeared. But curiosity and a certain sympathy for the monster's sorrow made him wish to speak to the monster first. He approached the tremendous being. He dared not raise his eyes again to the monster's face, so frightening and unearthly was its ugliness.

"If you wanted forgiveness," said the captain, "you should have thought of it long ago and not pushed your diabolical vengeance this far!"

"And do you think," said the demon, "that I did not feel agony and remorse for what I did?" The monster pointed to Frankenstein. "He did not suffer a thousandth of the agony that I suffered performing those hellish deeds. A frightful selfishness hurried me onward, while my heart was poisoned with remorse. Do you think the groans of Clerval were music to my ears? My heart was made for love and sympathy. And when it was made, by misery, to feel hatred, I suffered tortures you cannot imagine.

"After the murder of Clerval, I returned to Switzerland heartbroken. I pitied Frankenstein. My pity amounted to horror. I abhorred myself. But when I discovered that he, the creator of my life and my torments, dared to hope for happiness—that he, having destroyed my wife, was about to find joy in his own—then envy and bitterness filled me with rage. I wanted revenge, and I remembered my own threat to be with him on his wedding night. I could not help myself. Yet afterward, I was no longer miserable. I had cast off all feeling, all anguish. Evil thenceforth became my good. Having gone so far, I had no choice but to adapt myself to the plan I had begun. And now it has ended. There is my last victim!"

At first the captain was touched by the things the monster said. But he remembered Frankenstein's warning about the monster's powers of persuasion, and he grew angry again.

"Wretch!" said Captain Walton. "How dare you come here to whine over the destruction you yourself have caused? You are indeed a fiend!"

"No," whispered the monster softly. "You are wrong. But I do not seek pity. I shall never find sympathy. I never did, even when I was virtuous. How I longed for someone to overlook my outward form and return my love. Then, I had high thoughts of honor and loyalty. But now crime has lowered me beneath the meanest animal. No guilt, no misery can be found as great as mine. So how could I seek for sympathy? I am content to suffer alone as long as I live and to die with curses flung at my memory. I cannot believe I am the same creature whose thoughts were once full of beauty and kindness. But it is so. The fallen angel becomes a devil.

"Yet, while I destroyed Frankenstein's life, I did not satisfy my own desires. I still wanted love and fellowship, but always, all my life, everyone has spurned me. Why does man not hate Felix, who drove me out? Or the father who shot me when I saved his child? But no. People hate only me, the miserable, the abandoned, a thing to be kicked, spurned, and trampled on.

"But it is true that I am a wretch. I have drawn my creator to his ruin. But do not fear. I shall cause no more terror. I shall seek the most northern place of the globe. I shall collect my funeral pyre, light it, and throw myself upon its fire. The flames will consume me, and my ashes will blow out to sea so that no man, seeing my remains, can learn from them how to construct another such as I. I will no longer be miserable, no longer see the sun or stars or feel the winds play on my cheeks. Light, feeling, and sense will pass away. Damned as I am, where can I find peace except in death? Years ago, I should have wept to die. But no longer," said the monster sadly and solemnly. "Farewell. Farewell to you, the last human being whose eyes will ever see me. And Frankenstein, my creator, farewell."

As he said this, the monster leaped from the cabin window onto an ice raft that lay close to the ship. The captain could do nothing but stare after the monster, who was soon borne away by the waves and lost in darkness and distance.